DANDELION DAUGHTER

Dandelion Daughter

A NOVEL

Gabrielle Boulianne-Tremblay

TRANSLATED FROM THE FRENCH BY
ELI TAREQ EL BECHELANY-LYNCH

ESPLANADE BOOKS
THE FICTION IMPRINT AT VÉHICULE PRESS

Published with the generous assistance of the Canada Council for the Arts, the Canada Book Fund of the Department of Canadian Heritage, and the Société de développement des entreprises culturelles du Québec (SODEC).

Canada SODEC Québec

Canada Council   Conseil des arts
for the Arts   du Canada

Cover design by David Drummond
Set in Adobe Minion and Filosofia by Simon Garamond
Printed by Marquis Imprimeur

Originally published as *La fille d'elle-même*
by Marchand de feuilles © 2021
English translation copyright © Eli Tareq El Bechelany-Lynch 2023
Dépôt légal, Library and Archives Canada and the
Bibliothèque national du Québec, first trimester 2023

LIBRARY AND ARCHIVES CANADA CATALOGUING IN PUBLICATION

Title: Dandelion daughter : a novel / Gabrielle Boulianne-
Tremblay ; translated by Eli Tareq El
Bechelany-Lynch.
Other titles: Fille d'elle-même. English
Names: Boulianne-Tremblay, Gabrielle, 1990- author. | Tareq El
Bechelany-Lynch, Eli, 1994- translator.
Description: Translation of: La fille d'elle-même.
Identifiers: Canadiana (print) 20230161367 | Canadiana (ebook)
20230161618 | ISBN 9781550656183
(softcover) | ISBN 9781550656251 (EPUB)
Classification: LCC PS8639.R4507 F5513 2023 | DDC C843/.6—dc23

Published by Véhicule Press, Montréal, Québec, Canada

Distribution in Canada by LitDistCo
www.litdistco.ca

Distribution in the U.S. by Independent Publishers Group
ipgbook.com

Printed in Canada on FSC® certified paper.

For Thérèse, my gracious one,
who dances among the stars

For all my disappeared
trans sisters and brothers

For little Gabrielle, who didn't think
she would live past sixteen

I come from the large country of my childhood
With its tender gardens,
its streams of innocence.
I come, heartbroken, from a family
Within which I lived in a corner,
Half silence, half girl.

MARIE LAFORÊT
Emporte-moi (Take Me Away)

Tell me it's not normal to arrive at a bar and to grab the throats of others, inspecting the contours for the possible presence of an Adam's apple

(they aren't Adam's apples, they're Eve's apples)

tell me instead that under the influence of alcohol and the pressure from your dude friends who told you that the person you were checking out isn't a woman but a man in a dress, that in your fragile masculinity, it's shame that makes you obscene

so then tell me it's not normal that the police come to the bar with flashlights to inspect our papers, that in the laughter that escapes their uniforms there's our terror of dying on the spot

so then tell me it's not normal that in the rush of the bull, the waitresses turn on us, red, telling us that we're an insult to women, because as sluts in wigs we only know how to live at night, and we always have to look for a cab in the snow

so then tell me it's not normal to finally be wooed for once in our lives and to then be told, "you should come back and see me once you've had the operation so that we can try out your new vagina." it's true that you are the first to love us without feeling shame, that you've carried our struggle at arm's length, it's true that we owe our new lives to you, definitely not to ourselves

so then tell me it's not normal to be loved at night in between beers and joints, but not in the day, it's another girl you love, because you aren't sure, in the end, but that we'll see you happy a month later

so then tell me it's not normal to not want to get up when the doctor calls us by our dead name through the CLSC speakers, and tantalized with fear, we advance in disgrace

so then tell me it's not normal to say, "hide your penis, beautiful, if you want me to come," that we too never thought we could be desired for our beauty, for our whole selves

so then tell me it's not normal that you take the time to specify that you aren't gay if you sleep with us, you aren't teaching us anything new, but definitely don't tell us you are gay if you sleep with us

so then tell me it isn't normal to spend Christmas Eve alone at home, that each Christmas is a planned suicide, but that the balconies are never high enough and our cats understand the urge to hang ourselves

so then tell me it's not normal to be told that you're looking for a real woman to build something with (that when *you're talking about biological women, you're talking about vegetables)*

so then tell me it's not normal for journalists with a wide readership to publish rubbish about us in order to wipe themselves clean on the suffering of others

so then tell me it's not normal that you think it's right and good and lovely to take the trouble to tell us when it's going wrong that, in the end, it's because you wanted to pick up a cisgender woman at the bar, a non-trans woman

so then tell me it's not normal to use MTF to speak about us, male to female, man/woman, shemale, creature, deviant

so then tell me it's not normal to not be able to access our own bank accounts by phone because our voice doesn't correspond to the administrative gender that hasn't yet been changed

so then tell me it's not normal to lose our job and our apartment because no more job to pay the rent and we have to end up in the street or even maybe walk them

tell me instead that trans people will experience love and that we will no longer have to fight for our rights and our dignity

tell me instead that we won't get raped, that we won't die and be left in a ravine, found two weeks later, and misgendered even at our funeral by our parents who never really understood tell me instead that it's possible to see you love past the binary

tell us instead that the trans women who fought back did not die in vain

talk to us about love

talk to us about respect

but especially, if you don't understand, then talk to us

The red-bricked school makes me think of a large heart beating in the centre of the village. Today is my first day of school. It's the first time that I get to see the inside. The school is surrounded by poplar trees, guardians that sway in the wind in hypnotic movement. My group goes deeper into the schoolyard. We've just arrived but I'm already searching for places I can hide. There's a space reserved for dodgeball and another for hopscotch. The playground lines are freshly painted and we're warned to be careful with our shoes. The school is an old convent with a giant crucifix on the facade.

I enter the school. Stunned by the wall of unending mint-green lockers, I think that one day they might hide me. Lines of horizontal ceiling lights heat the white and black tiles. It feels like I'm walking on a giant chessboard. I'm afraid of getting taken by the queen. I'm wearing black leather shoes with a small heel that my mom spent a fortune on for the occasion. When we chose them, I told her that they fit. I was too scared of the saleswoman's intimidating look. My first lie. When I finally told my mom they weren't comfortable, she looked at me for a long time.

"I don't have the receipt anymore so you're going to have to deal with them this year. It's okay. You'll just walk a little slower," she told me as she reapplied her lipstick in the rear-view mirror before opening the car door onto my first day of school.

An acrid smell of detergent spreads and mixes with the dampness of hallways and rooms not aired all summer. I'm standing beside Olivier, my older brother. I'm holding his hand. I'm worried about crushing his bones. I'm worried that the excitable current of children will carry me away. We head to the gymnasium for a welcome ceremony.

After the principal's speech, we find out who our teacher will be. Martine. I like her already: her brown curls bouncing on her shoulders, her red cheeks, her small upturned nose that makes her look like she's on top of things. She's pretty with her tailored suit and her long waterslide legs. She's wearing white polka-dot tights. I find she looks like a Dalmatian. This makes me laugh and I chuckle during her introduction. I can't keep it inside my mouth. She looks at me. She smiles.

My brother is entering grade three. He speaks, in a laid-back way, with his friends. I'm jealous of his ease. Unlike me, this isn't the biggest day of his life. He seems pleased to be reunited with his friends. He makes his way, like a fish, among the other students. I don't know whom to turn to. All the kids in my class look shy, eyes fixed on the floor. Somehow, I'm still the shyest. There's this small stocky boy ahead of me. Summoning up my courage, I go to introduce myself. I take small painful steps. His name is Mathias. Dressed in clashing patterns, he looks like wallpaper. He cracks his knuckles, fiddles continuously with his hands, puts them in his pockets, takes them out. He looks like he's going to perform a magic trick and suddenly pull a rabbit out of his pocket. No one has come to see me and no one tries to talk to him either. I get a little closer. I watch his shoes with him, his gaze a little lost. When he finally notices me, he welcomes me like a good friend back from a long trip.

It's the first time I approach someone outside my family. It makes my bangs sticky with sweat. This might be my chance to talk to someone I don't know who seems just as shy as me. My mom clearly wants to see me make a friend in my too-tight shoes because she waits around until Mathias smiles at me. As she watches, I shed my reputation as a feral child who hides under the table anytime anyone comes over to visit. When I can't hide inside, I hightail it out of the house and into the woods round back. The branches are hands that propel me forward. I feel supported in my flight. The stinging scratches left behind are marks of love, I suppose.

Facing Mathias, I can't hide the trembling of my legs or my lips. I stutter and launch myself into long and clumsy sentences. He puts a hand on my shoulder and it immediately calms me. I should invite Mathias over so he can calm my mom and dad when they're fighting.

I'm shocked I managed to detach myself from my mom's skirt. I ask Mathias, "Do you want to be my best friend?"

The words whistle through my teeth in a voice more high-pitched than that of most boys my age. I breathe a sigh of relief. I did it. Hooray! I'm surprised and relieved;

these are the first words I've spoken outside my house. He responds immediately. I thought he would at least take the day to think it over. Things are happening quickly and my heart races every time Mathias wipes his nose on the sleeve of his turtleneck. There are no classes today; it's a special day. Dodgeball and hopscotch for everyone. Mathias and I rush to the playground, the sun warming our meeting. We have summer in our throats.

My mom wants to bring me to the village hairdresser. I make a fuss in the car by kicking the back of her seat every two seconds. She doesn't say a word. Angrily looks at me in the rear-view mirror. I'm chasing my own thunderstorm.

I don't want to leave the car. She removes my seatbelt and pulls me out by my overall straps. "Oh, stop being such a nuisance. Don't you want to start off the new year fresh? You're going to have a nice mushroom haircut like everyone else. Otherwise, what kind of impression would that give of us?"

At lunchtime, we head to the hairdresser's, which is in a basement. It's a funny place. When I walk in, the smell of hairspray burns my nostrils. Three chairs, one of which is waiting for me. The chairs in the back are occupied by two women reading magazines with massive round blow dryers covering their heads. It looks like they're going to be abducted by aliens. There's a door at the other end of the room leading to Gisèle the hairdresser's house. On a zebra print shelf, miracle products promise a transformative experience. There's something for everyone's wants, everyone's needs. I open the bottles, charmed by their smells.

There's a poster displaying the newest, most popular haircuts. My mom points to a little blond boy on one of the posters. "Give him a Nick Carter haircut, he'll be cute as all that. I'll come back to pick him up in two to three hours if it isn't a bother. I have to run some errands in town."

I'm stunned that my mom would leave me for so long. At my age, trapped in a chair, three hours is an eternity. She kisses my head before leaving.

The hairdresser has rings on all her fingers which come alive like centipedes. Her rings are silver, in the shape of hearts, arrows, one set with a diamond, another with amethyst, the rest engraved with her children's names. My hair strands are seized, one after the other, between heart and arrow. The scissors chomp my hair. I watch the strands fall, my eyes obstructed.

"Don't make that face, little guy. It's going to grow back anyway."

Gisèle goes to get a cigarette from her purse. She sets down her scissors. Lights up. A cloud soon appears above our heads. Gisèle asks one of the other women to open a window. A small guillotine window. When she turns my chair in its direction, I count the number of people passing by outside. We can only see their shoes or their sandals walking past. I imagine that the shoes and sandals are bodiless, the bodies at home resting. We'll never know.

Sometimes when she's in front of me, my nose almost presses up against her large breasts. I try to move my head. She warns me not to move, otherwise my haircut won't be even. When she brings her face close to mine to cut the top, she squints her eyes, closes one, checks if she's done well. She has the intensity of a huntress. She stands for a while in front of my face. Her fingers smell like Alberto mousse and cigarettes. "You look like an angel." I smile at her. I want to count each freckle on her face. I like counting. I ask her how many heartbeats we are given before we die.

"That's a big question for such a little person."

She takes a second to think about it. She looks at the ceiling as though the answer to my question is hidden there.

"I don't know, but when I think about it, it makes my heart pound faster, so let's cool our jets, eh?"

Gisèle keeps a bobby pin between her pursed lips. They're plum coloured and make her skin look green. Probably why people gossip that she's a witch. They say she's a husband thief, a home-wrecker. I can't see any danger because we exchange smiles and conspiratorial looks in the mirror. The other day at church, she sat at the back, alone, at the periphery of everyone's thoughts, almost forgotten. After the communion, my dad went to talk to her. Standing in front of the confessional booth, he tucked a fallen strand of hair behind her ear. She smiled. Her eyes bore into his. My mom always insists that she, and not my dad, bring me to the hair salon.

I look at my hair on the floor. A blond cloud splayed open. Even though I'm having a nice time with the hairdresser, I can sense a feeling of dread creeping in. I feel like I've lost a limb. I have the exact same haircut as the little boy on the poster. I don't look like myself. I look like someone else. I have the same haircut as Nick Carter. I could be his double if the Backstreet Boys ever needed a replacement. Gisèle takes off my black cape with magisterial flare.

"Tada!" I'm not me. I'm someone else. I don't recognize myself in the mirror. I keep touching my hair while she goes to check on the ladies at the back of the salon. She lights another cigarette. I pass my fingers through the few long strands left, then through the shaved area. She flattened my femininity, a forest of trees uniformly cut, leaving only the stumps. From now on, I'll be afraid to wash my hair because I'll have to pass my hands over the coarse short hairs that bristle against my fingers.

"I like your mom and all but you'll have to remind her that I'm not a babysitter," Gisèle tells me. "You can also tell her that she can pay me at the end of the month, that's no problem. It's been a good month, so I'm not stressed."

Another two hours of waiting before she comes back. One of the women leaves before my mom returns and another client arrives. I spend the time imagining what the witch's lair looks like upstairs. There are probably men sleeping, victims of her spells. The missing husbands. The casualties of love. I spend two hours daydreaming about the long and radiant hair of the girls in my class and wonder why boys have to keep their hair short. I wish I had Rapunzel hair.

My mom brings us to the beach. It takes her an eternity to leave the house. Olivier and I wait for her with our shovels, our buckets, our multi-coloured towels. She has to double-check the windows are actually closed and locked even if she already knows they are. She's worried that something might get in while we are gone. She says that if it rains, it could flood the house. I imagine our little house adrift on the Saint-Lawrence River.

After the windows, it's time to check the oven, then the sink. We've been hanging around for ten minutes, and pretty soon, we'll start to take root in the garden. There's no question of leaving before she's put her hands on the stovetop elements at least five times. I wonder what would happen if she happened to forget to turn off one of the burners. She passes her hands under the faucet to try and find a drop, the single herald of a disaster. This carousel, or ritual, I don't yet know what to call it, isn't sufficient. She comes over, looking distraught. "Drop your towels and your buckets in the car and go check if everything is okay in the house."

We have to wage a war against an invisible threat. Olivier and I understand there's no reason to be worried. The faucet handles are so tightly shut that it's impossible to turn them. Suddenly, I'm struck by the idea of retrieving her Polaroid camera. By the flash of the device, I decide to photograph each window, each door, each lock, and everything else that worries my mom. I head back out with a dozen photos in my hands. I hand them to her. My mom is surprised.

"You can look at the pictures if you think you haven't shut something."

My mom scolds me. "Why did you waste all those photographs? They were for the beach."

I remain frozen. She comes to her senses. "It's okay. I trust you. If anything happens, it'll be your fault."

She puts the photos in her purse. Her thank-you struggles to pass through her lips, but it's there, a tear in her eye.

The river brings me its invigorating benediction. I feel myself returning to life as I enter the water. I take in deep salty breaths. I hold them jealously inside me, they allow me to float. It's the only thing that can appease my fiery temperament. Beneath the afternoon sun, Olivier and I swim to the point of trembling, to the point of alarming blue lips. We get out to warm up, but we always go back in. I let myself drift along on my back. I am an ice floe that doesn't need a shore. I don't need anything other than this summer warmth on my face, in contrast to the rest of my body, submerged and frigid. The chills tighten my skin. I feel stripped of everything.

The only time I'm certain that no one will bother us is at this moment, swimming. We can relax without worrying about arrow-sharp words and vindication. No kid would want to dive into such icy waters. What other kid prefers frostbite to the comfort of a crowded municipal pool? I feel audacious. It gives me the feeling that I have control over them. Who do we think we are, being from here, to be so immune to the cold?

The seagulls drop their complaints and weave the blue of the sky with their immaculate white. I follow one with my eyes while continuing to float. Their complaints are distorted because of the water in my ears. They sound like the soft, warm beats of a drum, or it might be my own heart that I hear. I'm surprised by my heart, which allows me to do aquatic pirouettes, to swim, to love too many boys at once.

I bicker with my brother. He wants to be the king of the ocean. I climb up onto his shoulders and rub against his buzzed head with my knuckles to create an unpleasant heat. He hates when I do this, but I know that this way I can get what I want. We get out of the water for a bit. I can no longer feel my feet. I bury them in the scalding blond sand. I take some in my hands and pour it onto my still shivering thighs. It sparkles. Olivier makes sand castles. Together, we search for objects on the shore to use as decorations. We head all the way to the groves on the outskirts and come back with branches, stones, small shells, or pieces of coloured glass smoothed by the tide.

My mom has chosen a spot to sit. She has a large straw hat that creates a shadow across her shoulders and a bit over her chest. She looks like a parasol that won't stop talking. She takes out the radio and puts on a Joe Dassin Greatest Hits cassette. He'll be the soundtrack to our summer. She's madly in love with him, humming his songs at all hours. She says that the song "Dans les yeux d'Émilie" was written for her because her name is also Émilie. "At the Rec centre, your dad and I didn't know how to say that we loved each other. Joe Dassin started playing and we danced together. I took it as a sign. Olivier, listen to me, I'm telling you something. So, that's it, we kissed without our parents knowing."

Kissing becomes for me, as of this moment, a way to keep things close to me, a way to make sure they don't disappear. I have the sudden urge to kiss my bed and every tree in the forest. I'm lulled by Joe's warm and enveloping voice. Only he knows how to calm me. His songs wrap around me like a quilt. I imagine my mom one day dating him. He would talk to us about the world he sees and lives, thanks to his touring on the other side of the ocean. I could tell everyone that Joe Dassin is my dad (after all, he's here more often than my actual dad) and everyone would admire me for it, everyone would want to know what it's like being Joe Dassin's daughter.

In the meantime, Joe replaces Joel, my dad. When the chorus starts, my mom takes me by the hands and we dance together in the sand. She loses her hat. This dance, she would never admit, is a sort of invocation for my dad to come work in the village as a foreman instead of exiling himself in that faraway land, the North Shore, as a forestry worker. My mom is still dancing. This is the way I love her, when she no longer lets herself be knocked down by storms and she smiles.

She smears her frail body with suntan lotion. She has gotten thinner; I notice because her collarbone is sticking out. A perfume of heavenly ylang-ylang, sweet roses, and rich coconut charms my nostrils. The waves of her chestnut hair cascade onto her shoulders and then fall gently to the middle of her back. When she's done, I ask her if she can put some on me.

"You'll smell like a girl."

I don't care. It's my turn to be bathed in it. Oiled up like this, my mom makes me think of opals flashing in all their fire. She is the most precious treasure on the beach.

Look at her, that's my mom. I can collect sea shells to listen to what the ocean will whisper in my ear, but I will always prefer my mom's voice. A second later, she's deep in thought and I know that I should return to the water. She's almost in a vegetative state. If my mom is a house, she's deserted, her furniture sleeping under plastic tarps.

A man approaches my mom. He's tall, he has a large back, he's wearing sky-blue Bermuda shorts, and a lemon-yellow shirt. He's hard to miss. He's taken the liberty of shaking his towel in the wind and placing it near hers. He settles in. She doesn't seem to react. After some time, she takes off her hat, sits back down, and starts chatting with him. The conversation gets animated. My mom comes back to life, possessed by grandiose gestures. She gesticulates as though she's drowning in her happiness.

When we come out of the water for good to join them, she announces that she met a horticulturalist and we should be excited because our apple trees will finally flower again.

This is how Bernard pierces our lives. His salt-and-pepper hair makes him look older. He looks like a snow owl, with his bulging amber eyes and his hooked nose. He comes by every weekend to take care of our wild apple trees. He cuts off the dead or rotten branches that hinder the trees' growth. He finishes by spraying the leaves with a fine mist that stinks up the orchard for several minutes. It makes my nose wrinkle. Bernard waves at me. Every time he arrives in his old, noisy truck, like right out of some black-and-white era, my mom emerges from her upstairs bedroom as if from a dream. She flies down the stairs, puts on a light jacket, and goes outside while waving her hand. Her welcome is as warm as those she usually reserves for the holidays. She pours herself a coffee, sits down in a wicker chair on the porch, and watches him work. A satisfied smile lights up her face.

Sometimes, she makes her way to the apple trees, where their whispers are secret. It's time for the harvest. Olivier and I climb the trees to shake the branches and make the apples fall into large nets on the ground.

Sometimes my mom helps Bernard. She puts her hands on the ladder and he puts a laugh at the edge of every one of his sentences. It's sweet to see her like this. She bakes tarts to thank him, and we get to have the leftover filling. We delight in our mom's good mood, as she falls in the apples.

She talks about him, always saying "Him," never calling him by his first name. It's weird, because, at school, we're told that only God can be referred to in this way.

The euphoria of a new person in our lives fades quickly. When we do our errands in the village, the looks weight us down. At the grocery store, the owner talks about Bernard to my mom while he scans our purchases at the cash. "He has an American accent, your horticulturalist. Is he hiding away here because he committed a crime over there, huh?" "How come his truck is always at yours?" "He's not with you today. That's pretty rare." My mom rolls her eyes and sighs. And I'm worried because, suddenly, I'm ashamed to be her kid. The owner doesn't try very hard to hide his smile.

My mom loses her opal radiance as the days go by. She takes refuge in a new silence, more and more drawn out. In the schoolyard, we are told our mom is a slut because a man comes over all the time. The little vipers at school won't let it go. The horticulturalist is blamed. He doesn't have a wife. "You don't come to church anymore because you know you're going to burn, eh?" "Your mom is a whore, which makes you a bastard." "Maybe your father isn't even your real father."

It sounds dirty. Red. Bones cracking. Bloody flags. Get into it. Sink deeper, rush headlong into the circle of girls having fun under the boys' astonished gazes.

I'm pushed. Shoved. They take hold of my arms. A girl

slaps me before I even see her approaching. She'll never be my friend, that's for sure. Their laughter splits their faces, filled with hatred. "Wash your hands after touching that fleabag." The birds fly away so as not to be witnesses, scared of the young wolves' synchronized cry. I feel like biting them and giving them my rage. Let them try to spend a quiet day after, with this rage that grips your heart and makes you want to swing out a window.

My eyelids shut as a massive shudder passes through me. I push the first boy in my way. He falls onto the asphalt. It wasn't on purpose. I just wanted him to move out of my way so I could pass. This boy, a ridiculed criminal in front of the girls, this image of him vulnerable, trying to figure out what just happened, is delectable. There he is crying. No one says another word.

"Leave me alone!"

The veins in my neck protrude and I feel my heartbeat in my temples, my vision blue with violence.

Banned from recess for a week and a call to my mom. It's not a huge punishment. I prefer staring at the white wall of the detention room to being among the others. I plan something to draw my mom out of her sadness. I want to bring my dad back into their bed.

One day, the rumour that my mom is in love with Bernard the horticulturalist travels down Highway 138 and makes it all the way to my dad's ears. On the phone, my mom tries to smother a thunderstorm. She pleads with my dad to understand that Bernard is just a good friend. She closes the door of her bedroom and I no longer hear anything. Her tears snake around my ankles and I cry in turn.

I'm with Olivier in his room playing with animal figurines. A pickup enters the yard in a fury. I wonder why Bernard is coming over so late. But then, I recognize my dad's forest-green pickup. The truck makes its way into the yard and stops in front of the entrance, the dust stirred up as it passes. My mom exits the house, not in a hurry, as though she were psyching herself up to dive into the cold water of a lake. I can see another storm forming. At first, all is calm. We barely sense the arrival of the rain in our bones. If we struck a match, we would cause an explosion in seconds. Their voices gain strength. I'm trying to figure out what they're saying, but their voices become superimposed, the echo of a cannon.

We hurry over to the porch. My mom orders us to go back inside. I feel like pissing myself. It's the first time my dad looks like a monster, his rage deforming his features. I hide behind Olivier to protect myself. I grip his shirt with all my strength. My mom moves closer to my dad, still behind the wheel, as he lowers his window. He doesn't want to leave the car. He pushes my mom back by shouting. She slumps to the ground. Gets up right away. Then hurries in front of the truck to block my dad's way.

"I'm going to run you over if you don't move aside," he shouts.

Where are the tender words of love? My dad left them on the North Shore.

The neighbours turn on their porch lights, just as surprised as we are. My mom doesn't move.

"Stop, Dad!" Olivier and I shout out in chorus.

Shaking with uncontrollable jolts, I cry words already dead.

Mom puts her hands on the hood. "Let's see you try it."

He doesn't stop yelling at her. He starts calling her a whore, just like the kids at school. He does a manoeuvre to avoid her by accelerating and my mom falls down again. This time, she doesn't get up. The tires squeal onto the 138 and the truck disappears in the night. Émilie and Joel's love just went out. Her eyes are filled with tears and things she isn't telling us. She gets back up, takes us by the hand, and brings us back to the house.

"Go to bed, you nosy bunch," she shouts at the neighbours still on their doorsteps, hunched over like vultures. "There's nothing left to see here!"

She slams the door behind her. All three of us settle down on the couch.

"My loves. You're going to have to be strong." She strokes our heads, and anxiety germinates in mine.

"Joe Dassin is dead. Right, Mom? Because if not, I think he would take care of you."

My mom cries and chuckles at the same time. She presses us hard against her, and the fatigue that follows big emotions puts us to sleep.

Bernard hasn't come over since the incident. It's been four weeks since my mom has become immersed in her silences, and sometimes I catch her crying in front of the pan or while slicing bread. She looks in the direction of the apple trees, wipes her cheeks. Is she thinking of Bernard? She wipes the counters incessantly by going over the same spot a dozen times. Maybe in the hopes of erasing what happened in the yard several weeks ago? Autumn smells of Windex and Comet. It makes me nauseous.

While in the pasta aisle at the grocery store, I see Bernard, basket on his arm. He hasn't seen me. He looks tired, with dark circles under his eyes. My mom is at the end of the aisle. She pretends to look for something in the pockets of her beige pants, in her leather purse, she searches for courage in the pocket of her jacket. It seems to me like my mom is finally alone. She opens her mouth and then shuts it right away. They look at each other from either end of the aisle, now silent. They measure each other up, like two dogs with two different owners when they cross paths. She doesn't look happy to see him. They don't say a word to each other. In the grocery store, a thick layer of ice forms between them. She changes aisles when they cross paths. So much seems to want to burst out from Bernard's tight lips. He looks very pale in his navy-blue coat. His back is arched like an old tree. He shows his apprehension by approaching slowly. I would like to hear them speak. I head towards him when my mom has her back turned. Breaking my neck to look him in the eyes, I ask, "Why is my mom avoiding you?"

"Because she loves me and it's not possible."

I rejoin my mom at the cash. Leaving the grocery store, I ask her, "Do you still love Dad?"

She doesn't respond.

The following autumn, we have apples that taste like nothing.

When my mom has Bianca—one of her old high school friends—over, she always sits right beside the phone in case my dad calls. Bianca is a magazine model. She travels a lot. Every time she's back in Québec, she makes sure to see my mom. Her hair is jet black, and when she wraps her long arms around me, it feels like I am being plunged into the night. Her manicured nails drum against my back. Then, I sit at the table to draw, watching her from the corner of my eye.

Mom spins the black cord of the handset around her fingers and they chat. Her laughter doesn't ring true to the moment, there's a delay. Bianca chides her for not listening. "Joel will come back to you. Men leave, they come back, they leave again. They're like waves. You've gotta know how to ride the current," sings Bianca, twice divorced, the shame of the village.

She clicks her spoon against her cup. Her fluorescent pink nails are the only touch of colour in this beige living room. Mom decides after some time to move spots, farther away from the phone.

I'm downtown with my mom. Olivier isn't with us because he's at his friend's for the weekend. We're taking a walk. Joe Dassin played the whole car ride over. Dad is coming back. He called yesterday. We are feverish. I'm worried because I'm not sure if he's returning out of love or to strike her with a bunch of insults. She wants to buy a new set of cutlery for having guests over. She has a lost, faraway look and trembling hands. Her bottom lip is squeezed between her teeth. She bites it incessantly. I think back to the incident: the slammed doors, the tears, the truck that took my dad far from us.

When we arrive at the gift shop, the owner, Hélène, finishes sweeping away the autumn leaves from the entrance of the shop, Je me souviens. Hélène invites us in and reminds my mom that she's entitled to a special discount because she shops there so often.

We have dozens of cutlery sets to choose from. When we turn the utensils in the light to examine them up close, they cast refractions on the walls. I let myself become hypnotized by the patterns of light. My mom inspects them from all angles as though they were the most important things in the world. In her small floral blouse, she has a severe look that repulses me because it's often followed by an argument. A knife in hand, she considers the blade for a good minute. I wonder why she's so interested in this mundane kitchen knife. Then she slides the blade across the skin of her thumb. I think it's a joke but then a thin red line appears on her skin. I stifle a sob, stunned. She notices me. Gives me a nervous smile. Am I dreaming?

I head over to the owner to get help, but my mom grabs me by the sleeve of my turtleneck. I turn back. She puts her index finger to her lips to tell me not to say anything. She releases her grip. Cutlery set under her arm, she pays as though nothing happened. She chats with Hélène. "If you want an apple pie, I'll bring you one next time."

During this time, a small red stain appears on the coat pocket where she slid her injured hand. She asks if I want some brown-sugar fudge that Hélène made. I say yes out of politeness.

We return to the car. She places the cutlery set beside me. I still sit in the back because I'm not big enough to sit up front. She drives with her cut, which is still bleeding. The blood ripples out like snakes eating the steering wheel.

"Mom, you're bleeding."

I find it odd that I have to remind her that she hurt herself not even five minutes ago.

"Oh, it's nothing serious. See?" She puts her thumb in her mouth to stop it from bleeding. I open the window to get some air and to alleviate the urge to throw up.

At home, she takes care of her cut, disinfects it, puts on a bandage, and starts pulling out the ingredients she needs for supper. Together, we chop the peppers, the carrots, and the celery for the spaghetti sauce. I can't quite suppress the nausea that assailed me earlier at the gift shop. The rest of the time I spend daydreaming on the couch. My mom finishes putting the glasses on the table just as the guests arrive. We can no longer hear ourselves think.

I decide to go for a walk in the woods to restore my spirit. When I get back, a half hour later, my dad is sitting beside my mom on the couch, in between two friends. They're sharing a cigarette. Other guests play cards at the low living room table. My mom seems preoccupied. She wipes her tears when she sees me and invites me into her arms. Then, my dad encircles me. I scrutinize their eyes, searching for a sign of the people who took possession of their bodies and are playing at being Émilie and Joel.

My mom is doing extra hours at work. She leaves at the same time as us in the morning. She spreads peanut butter on our toasts and asks us to cut the bananas ourselves because she's in a rush. She blows us a kiss and hurries into the car.

Dad returns to the North Shore. When I talk about my parents almost never being at home, my friends look at me with doubt. Martine worries and takes me aside after the bell rings.

"If there's anything I can do, I'm here."

Just her presence reassures me; she's already doing a lot.

My mom doesn't have the time to play with us; she had to lift and clean the bodies of old people all day, had to manage a dementia crisis, and succumbed to at least one crying fit in the bathroom since getting home. Things are no longer going well between my dad and her. She spends hours on the phone with Bianca, who can't take it anymore.

I call Mathias and ask him if I can come over for supper this evening. When I get there, Rachel, Mathias's mother, gives us some salsa and chips while we wait. We finish the bowl quickly. We sit down on the couch and watch cartoons. Rachel kisses Mathias on the forehead; he kisses her back. I miss my mom's kisses. Benoît, Mathias's father, is repairing his motorbike in the yard. I also miss my dad. I think of him this evening, away deforesting, while he strikes at love with the intent of a clear cut.

Mathias and I are transfixed by the cross at the top of the mountain, which is illuminated on this late afternoon in autumn. It is so brightly lit that you can't look at it for too long. The cross seems to float between the tops of the trees, which will soon lose their leaves. It seems like Jesus doesn't sleep and is watching us. The sun starts to fall asleep. Our faces take on a golden glow. Being with Mathias causes an incredible sensation in my chest, more so because, soon, we're going to cross into the forbidden.

I once again look at the cross. Ask Jesus for forgiveness. But it's stronger than me. The village is calm. Not a cat, just the rumour of a dog happy to be playing outside. The smell of freshly mowed lawn. Our whistling breaths. The murmur of the poplars. The cold caress of rocks in our hands. Too late to turn back. The sun sets and leaves an orange wound on the horizon.

"It means that it's been a hot day and that tomorrow will be hot as well," I tell Mathias.

I can hear my grandmother telling me this. We extend our arms. Like stretched arcs. Without hesitation, I throw the first rock at the glass. Mom is screaming at Dad. A second rock. Dad is screaming at Mom. And a third rock. Dad wants to run Mom over with his truck.

It's the gymnasium window. Mathias throws them as well. I take a bigger rock, and this time I throw it with both my hands. The window explodes into shards and the pieces fall to the ground with magical clinks. The rock rolls and ends its trajectory in the middle of the gymnasium. It's soothing, the melody of shattered glass and torn silence. I want to continue with the other windows, at once to free their voices as well as the violent images that are on repeat constantly in my head. Mathias holds me back, stops me from throwing more rocks, because someone has approached the schoolyard. We have to leave. Escape in a puff of smoke. I don't know how to write about my struggles. I cope in whatever way I can.

We run. At the bend in the alley, my shoes with the smooth soles skid on the clay. I find myself on the ground. The sidewalk shreds my thigh and my right leg. Mathias pulls ahead. I lose sight of him. Just when I start crying, thinking I'm going to be caught, he picks me up. The race continues. My shin is bleeding. Drops of blood behind me, so as not to forget how to find the path back to the origin of my cry.

"You little shits, just wait till I catch you," someone screams as evening breaks. I give him the finger without turning around. Mathias grabs my hand and accelerates our pace. An electric current goes through my forearm and cuts my breath. I didn't realize how badly I'd been waiting for Mathias to touch me.

We rush into his house. Rachel and Benoît are at the movies. Mathias slams the door, locks it right away, and shuts the blinds. We ran as though we were in a zombie invasion. It's exciting and terrifying all at once. Intoxicated by the mad dash and the adrenaline, we collapse together.

What an adventure. If I could go through life like this without anyone seeing me, I could have the world at my feet.

To remove the grains of sand stuck in my cut, he uses a rag run under hot water. I panic. I don't feel anything. Is it the shock from the fall? This cut, I look at it from every angle—my knee, my leg—I have the feeling that my body isn't my own. "Am I really myself? It's like it's not even my leg."

Mathias scrutinizes me with a dubious look. He approaches and wipes the dust from my shirt. He looks at me again. "You really can't feel your leg? I'm pretty sure it's real blood. Wait, I'll taste it. Look!" He leans towards my knee. I start laughing. His turn to laugh heartily. It feels like I'm walking beside myself when I get up to sit on a chair. I would like to be able to feel this injury.

I'm worried that the sidewalk, like the neighbour's dog, will give me rabies. I imagine myself in a couple of minutes, frothing at the mouth. Sweat dripping down my temples, I ask, "How much time do I have left?"

"Come on, it's nothing. I'm taking care of it."

I feel like making more absurd remarks, just to hear him laugh like that again. He pours some peroxide on the cut, which creates a fascinating foam upon contact.

"Put some more on. It's fun."

Once again, I admire the emulsion of blood and foam, as though my knee has become a volcano.

He shows me a scar he got from falling off his bike. A half moon on his forearm. Mathias would therefore be the sky. I feel like kissing him. Curious sensations dance in the pit of my stomach.

Our successful mission makes me proud. I'm relieved for now, until the next blow. We high-five. His small canines stick out of his smile. His nice cheeks have turned pink with the effort it took to flee and they look like two apples ready to be picked.

"I like spending time with you."

It makes him smile. At my house, the following night, I can't fall asleep.

Every day, I try to get eliminated first during dodgeball so I can walk around the schoolyard instead. On the right side of the school, the side that gives onto the forest, near the wooden fence, bricks form a mound. The way they're placed resembles a staircase and gives me an idea. I climb them without much difficulty; I like climbing things. I tell myself that by using this pile, I can finally get to the other side of the fence. I'm so discreet that no one notices my absence, not even Martine. The echoes of the game reach me like relaxing music. With the fierce anticipation of vertigo, I try climbing the fence without anyone knowing.

The path snakes until it disappears into the belly of the forest. Fascinating and scary. I've been told that one evening a young and reckless boy, trying to be rebellious, took his father's ATV and died when he hit a tree at full speed. They also say that his ghost roves beneath the cedars, searching for other kids to bring to the afterlife.

In the evening, you can sometimes hear the roar of an engine. It's possible that it's the killer ATV, the sad ghost prince's steed. They say that if we don't go home before a certain hour, we will see it. The village kids don't mess around with this. Our very own boogie man. We're lucky to have such an original story. It's admirable that a boy tried to elude his parent's authority to explore the world along this trail. It inspires me. I'm going to do better; I'm not going to die in the middle of my mission. I will make it. I'll send my parents postcards to tell them I have not forgotten them, but that I'm happy to be far away from them. I will accomplish what he didn't. A feat they will talk about for generations.

My body is sucked up by the wind that rushes in from the path. I straddle the fence. I'm at the summit. Half in the schoolyard and half in a world to explore, filled with promise and redemption. The Indian summer coats my forehead in sweat. I take it as blessed approval. "Come," the trees murmur to me, "come."

But someone screams because they get the ball right in the face, and I jump. I lose my balance. As I fall, a piece of fence pierces my thigh. Lightning cuts through me. I feel this pain. It reassures me about the other pain that I didn't feel the other day. Much to my disappointment, I realize I've fallen back into the schoolyard.

My sweat goes cold, freezing my neck. For half a second, I was a holy effigy of otherworldly conquest. I'm angry with myself for not making it farther than the sad ghost prince. I feel ridiculous. I'm so mad that I feel like hitting myself. A crowd forms, curious, around the body that is no one's. Some students have furrowed brows; others guffaw. Will a day come when I'll no longer be a laughingstock? I dissolve into a clammy sweat.

Once in the principal's office, I suffer through his lecture. He has a white beard that makes me feel like I'm being preached at by that man in the clouds who we call God.

"But if there wasn't a barrier, there would have been no accident, sir. Why keep us captive like chickens?"

The principal is speechless. Martine adds to the sermon by saying that I could have been hurt badly. The muscles in her cheek jerk like a machine gun. I don't listen to them. I think of the euphoria I felt at the top of the fence. I want to feel that again. I want to line up those quarter seconds like beads of a necklace that would remind me that I'm alive.

One day, I will pass by the cedars and will become friends with other fugitives of my species. Nothing will stop us from digging into the earth to find refuge.

"I understand, I won't do it again, I promise (blah blah blah). I think it's time for me to go take care of my injury, no?"

The principal and Martine devolve into apologies; too absorbed by their reprimands, they forgot that I was hurt. Adults! You've got to always bring them back to reality.

I return to class with a bandage. I think about death. To die on school chairs, the sound of scissors devouring cardboard during crafts. I think about the fact that I would have had the most ridiculous death in the world. I think about the fact that it might be the last time I see the dust from the chalk that shines and floats in the blazing streak of the day, about Martine whom I didn't dare call out for when I fell, because I wanted to remain alone in my pain.

On Martine's desk, there's a statuette of Jesus that looks at me with nails fixed into his palms. Sooner or later, he will undoubtedly reveal that I was the one who broke the gymnasium window. They're still looking for the culprit. Embedding myself in a conversation between Martine and the principal, I slip in, out of nowhere, "It might not be someone from the school."

Jesus fixes me with his gaze. "I'm still holding myself upright. You're pathetic and you're a coward." I feel like crying.

I feel like my cut is going to open up between one heartbeat and the next, that it wants to talk to me. Maybe it'll find my words for me. I want to stick my fingers into the cut and discover how to live with parents who no longer love each other.

I wake up in the immaculate whiteness of an infirmary. I'm lying down, a cold cloth on my forehead. I am told I fainted on my desk. I'm weighed. I'm asked if I eat enough at home. Frozen meals, most of the time, improved with ketchup and pepper. I explain about my mom and dad, and add that the former is busy working doubles.

I'm handed an orange juice. The acidity gives me heartburn. She gives me a pill to relieve my pain. I've never swallowed a pill in my life. It's my first time. Usually, I take them away from others. Because of my failed climb, they've already named me the monkey who missed. Later on, it will be the little girl who missed. Always botched, never well made.

Mom was called when the accident happened and she comes to get us just before the end of classes so no one will notice us. She steps out of the car, still wearing her uniform.

"What am I going to do with you? And you." She looks at Olivier. "How is it that you aren't taking care of your brother?"

Olivier lowers his head.

"What am I going to do with you, my little one… I'm not going to be able to go to work without worrying. I'll always worry that I'll have to come back and get you. I'll also wonder: what might have happened today?"

Her voice breaks.

"Are you going to start climbing roofs and maim yourself while falling? Will we have to push you in a wheelchair? Now, you're going to have to start cooperating, give me a chance here. What am I going to do with you?"

Martine seems to be on the verge of interrupting. I don't respond. I don't know how to enter the world, how to be well behaved like the others who don't ruffle feathers. I cry.

"Eh? What are we going to do with you?"

We're going to do our best, Mom, we'll do our best.

When I go over to Mathias's, it's always special to see the buses leaving without me. We walk to his house while bickering happily. His basement is our favourite place to hang out. We play with the cushions from the old couch that stinks of mothballs. We make rafts with empty boxes. There's a place, near the hot-water tank, where things are pushed into a corner a bit haphazardly, threatening to fall at any second. His father's hockey equipment, his mother's tennis rackets and golf clubs, pell-mell. Rachel brings us grilled cheeses that she just made. After devouring the delicious meal, we give free rein to our imagination with chalk on the blackboard. Mathias's talent for drawing is undeniable. He succeeds in making me believe that the surrealist animals he's brought to life really exist.

When we play video games in the living room, he asks me why I always choose Princess Peach when we play Mario Kart. I tell him because she's blonde, she has blue eyes like me, and she's also pale. I envy her long silky mane and I too want to have pearls suspended from my earlobes.

"Okay, but she's a girl. Why don't you choose a guy?" he answers me, a little bit annoyed.

I tell him she looks more like me than the green dinosaur or the winged turtle. The uneasiness never lasts long. We're competitive and we have to concentrate to win.

I often lose when I play against him. He teases me with his victory. It's nice when he punches me in the shoulder. His mom asks us how we're doing. Something that mine never does; it makes a nice difference. She asks us in a gentle tone to go play outside. In any case, the cartridge in the console has gotten hot because we've played for so long. My mom would have raised her voice. I wonder if I could have two mothers. That would be great.

When we go inside to eat, the flavours jostle in my mouth and blow me away. The chicken melts so quickly that I tell myself, this must be what it's like to eat on top of the clouds. It calms my stomach, which is knotted from the stress of not hearing any news from my dad. This house is a peaceful haven. Those problems don't exist here. My dad left so quickly. I learn to appreciate moments as though they'll be my last.

One morning, I arrive in class and look for Martine. It's unusual for her to not be there before the students. The blinds are still shut. I try to open them. She always lets me do it. Mathias helps me. A woman enters the class. She looks like a crow with her glasses perched on her large nose, their arms attached by a silver chain that captures the light. She looks around the class, asking us to sit at our desks. An attendance sheet in hand, she asks us to raise our hand when she calls out our name. Dressed all in black, she competes with the village hairdresser for the title of witch. Actually, this woman looks like winter.

"My name is Christine. I'm replacing your teacher Martine for two weeks. She had a little bike accident. Sit down before the bell rings."

Mathias and I exchange a look. We know we're going to have a tough time with her.

Over the next few days, a cold settles over the classroom. No one dares ask questions. My classmate Melissa is given a taste of the witch's medicine. She asks her a question about an equation.

"Well, I don't know if there's anything Melissa could do to find the answer. I wonder if you're all like her…"

Melissa, red from embarrassment, will stay silent for the rest of the time that Christine is our substitute.

I do my best so that Christine, the crow, has no claim to my smile. I reserve it for Martine. I don't talk to her either. I have the impression that I'm going to get a smack on the back of the head when she passes behind me to survey our work. Every morning with Martine, we read a La Fontaine fable, but the regime of terror instated by Christine doesn't leave any space for this sort of activity. I worry about turning to stone if I look her in the eye. Mathias has the hiccups.

"Go wait in the hallway; you're disturbing the class, Mathias."

His hiccups can be heard through the door. Christine sees that I can't stop looking at the door, thinking of my friend who has been unjustly punished.

"Nose in your notebooks. Go on."

It's time for our class photos. We're in the gymnasium. I notice they installed new windows with grills. "To stop the awful attacks by those little troublemakers," the principal said to us before returning to his office.

We're sitting on long wooden benches. If someone moves, the whole row can tell right away. It feels like being on a boat to nowhere. Sitting with my hands on my knees, I feel ridiculous in the grey shirt Olivier gave me. The Mickey Mouse drawing is a little crackly from wear. Everyone else has overalls, turtlenecks, or neat cardigans. I try to hide the spaghetti sauce stains on the cuffs. I watch them, in their exuberant enthusiasm; I'd like to join them in their excitement, but instead, I'm terrified because I don't know how to smile for real. I'm happy when I break windows, when I climb fences to run away, when I get hurt and am cared for.

For the individual photos, the photographer asks me the worst thing: to smile. This time, I can't conceal myself in the fauna of faces belonging to smiling cherubs. I'm at the mercy of the creature who is watching me. The one that captures my sadness and, worse still, immortalizes it. The flashes follow one another.

"I can't let you leave until you give me your best smile, little guy. Think of a nice memory," the photographer tells me.

I search, I dig, the beach. I no longer see the photographer's face; it becomes an orange point that pulses. I am overcome with panic when I realize that I no longer know how to smile on command, not even pretend, and I don't have any memories that I can hang on to. I finish by giving him what he wants, a forced smile because it would have taken all my strength to offer him a real one.

A week later, our photos are handed out. The class is worked up. Christine lets us spend a mere ten minutes exchanging them. She places one of hers on each of our desks. What an insult. A photo to remind us that we won't get one of Martine. I look at my pictures. It looks like there's no one behind my blue eyes. I immediately recognize my mom in this sad absence. If only I had long hair, the picture would be better. In the end, I think I gave my best smile. And yet, all I see is a grimacing face twisted in pain. I don't want to give it to anyone. I'm ashamed. Mathias insists on having one. I make an exception. I look outside. The fence tempts me again. One day, I'll have my vengeance. I'll show them what I'm capable of.

Mathias gives me his photo. His cheeks are red, as though he were wearing makeup. It happens to him when he laughs. I immediately put the photo away in my agenda.

"Too bad we don't have a picture of Martine. She's really everyone's favourite teacher," I say loudly so that the crow hears me.

She raises her gaze from her notebook and fixes me with a furious glare.

At the end of the picture exchange, I rip her photo into pieces that I shove into my pocket to throw away later in the bathroom. Mathias sees me do it; he's a bit stunned but doesn't say anything. We go to his house after school to finish our level in the video game.

[58]

More and more often, my mom goes into town to visit old friends who've moved there. She often comes back smelling of alcohol. My anxiety is hard to manage. There's no point in trying to convince her to stay at home with us; it isn't possible to change her mind.

"Olivier is old enough to watch you."

I cry until I'm exhausted. I ask my brother, "Does Mom still love us?"

I have a terrible feeling that something might happen to her, especially when she staggers out of the car because she drank red wine, white wine, and Jack Daniel's.

"Don't touch my Jack," she tells us.

I tell myself that Jack is another man who makes her unhappy. I wait for her return by the solarium window. My brother channel-surfs. He often grinds his teeth; I have to remind him to stop. He keeps everything inside, that one. I end up falling asleep with my head on his thighs. When I wake up, before we go to sleep in our bedrooms, he strokes my hair.

My mom's fatigue weighs on our mornings. It's as though blocks of concrete have been hung from her rare smiles. From what my dad tells us on the phone, he's still on the North Shore in order to make more money for our family. Mom always has her coat on her back. It's become giant because she's gotten thinner. It looks like it could swallow her one day.

Mom gets ready for work and, unlike her usual self, she drags her feet.

"It looks like you're washing the floor with your feet," I tell her.

"Christ, can you help me a bit around the house?"

It's the first time that I hear my mom swear. It makes my legs hurt.

"If you could just pick up after yourselves, it would be nice to not always have to wipe your asses."

Olivier freezes up too. He was just buttering his toast. Mom lights a cigarette. "I'm going to be late because of you."

"What are we eating tonight?" asks Olivier.

"I don't know, make yourself whatever you want. I just don't have the time right now."

I think about Mathias's mom. I ask, "Mom, will you give us kisses this morning?"

She gets close to us and starts crying, her face in her hands. "I'm sorry, boys. Mom isn't in a good mood this morning."

She kisses me quickly on the forehead. I feel like crying but I no longer know how.

In the evening, Olivier asks me to get the potatoes from the basement. We're going to make a salmon pie, Mom's favourite, and there will be some left over for her when she gets home. I go down, not without fear of being attacked in the dark. It's a menacing place, both because it's cold and because there must be ghosts waiting patiently to grab my ankles from under the staircase.

The basement isn't renovated, which makes the place that much more unnerving. There's still that clay earth that turns to mud after heavy rain. My dad then has to take out the pump to push the water outside. The ground is sludgy and precarious. I think that one day, the house might sink like our words.

Barefoot on the cold clay, I walk through the faint glow of the low ceiling light bulb that's so old it flickers. I'm impatient to get to the potatoes, stored in a basket next to a cabinet where my dad stores pieces of wood. A musty odour floats in the air; it mixes with the smell of green shoots that sprout in the dark.

A creaking. I panic. I hurry to grab the bag of potatoes. Friction. A pile of stuff. The creaking becomes more insistent. It comes from the back of the basement, behind a thick nailed door. I feel like hightailing it out of the basement. However, I'm mesmerized by the creaking, by this door that moves more and more. When I open the door, something cries out and rushes furiously past my legs. The thing stops and I can finally make out what it is. It's a raccoon. For one long minute, we lock eyes. I ask it what it's doing there. It doesn't move. It's not terrified. It seems like it's waiting for something, like it wants to tell me something. I decide to look into the room. It's entirely dark. I open the door a bit more; some more light floods in. I tremble with my potatoes in hand. This room is outside of time. In the mirror on top of the workbench, I see myself with long hair, a dress, pearly nails, bracelets in every colour, I see myself and I can tell that I'm beautiful. "I'm a girl." The words leave my mouth and do not trouble me, rather they reassure me, even as I'm astonished. Olivier calls me from the kitchen. The raccoon is no longer there. A small window in the basement is open. I don't really understand what just happened. I just know that I feel a little bit lighter than when I entered the room, that everything I was holding in was finally able to see the light from the shadows.

At school, Olivier and I have a reputation; everyone thinks we're dirtbags because we come from the far edge of the village. They say that we don't have running water and that we have to bathe in the lake. So many rumours about one family. Sometimes, I tense up at the idea of going to class, just thinking about what else they'll make up about us.

When I wake up, I admire the rays of light that penetrate my blinds and warm my bed. When I open the window, the smell of lupine and roses adorns my mornings. I'm often the first to rise, but this time Olivier is up before me. I hear him washing dishes, moving a chair. The smell of toast and peeled oranges reaches me. My hunger deepens. I put on my Star Wars pyjamas and head downstairs. Olivier is preparing breakfast. He even made coffee for Mom, who's in the bathroom. The weekends are always more peaceful than the weekdays.

My mom gets to the kitchen, a smile on her face, and her rare good mood has me feeling like I'm floating.

"Look what's on the table."

It's honey, in a pot decorated with small flowers and a ribbon tied in a bow. I've never tasted honey before. I unscrew the lid. My mom watches me. It feels like Christmas. The liquid's viscosity impresses me; I watch it cover my toast and move with a slowness fragrant with flowers. Tasting it, I'm struck by the myriad sensations on my taste buds. It tastes like joy.

"It's good, eh?"

This moment imprints itself on my heart. This mother who spruces herself up for her children, who speaks to them softly. It's like finding the mother we had before the storm clouds gathered.

"Bernard gave us this. Isn't he kind?"

I don't know how to react. I feel like he does too much, but I content myself with smiling at my mom. I refuse to act like a killjoy. It's already exceptional that she's in such a good mood.

Monday, at school, they'll say to me, "Are you kidding? Honey has been around for a long time, come on, were you living under a rock?" "Oh that's right, you live in the forest." And much later on, when I'm a woman and I miss my mom, I'll buy myself a pot of honey.

It's time for indoor games. Martine walks around the classroom with her little nose in the air. She passes near me. I am the only boy who's in the girls' pink universe. My two friends—both girls—and I have a little house with pink shingles. Pink door. Pink stairs. At the beginning, the girls found it weird that I joined them. But with time, they got used to my presence. The boys especially look at me funny. Mathias doesn't come with me, even if he's tempted. He stays in his universe of big trucks. A whole life takes place in our little plastic home. I take care of watering the flowers on the lawn and I fall in love with the neighbour, Billy, a name chosen unanimously. He drives a Cadillac to work. Love stories are birthed on the second floor unbeknownst to the parents on the couch, who are watching TV. Secrets are buried under piles of laundry. One of my friends diligently organizes the Barbie clothes by colour. She yells at us if we have the misfortune of forgetting to put a piece of clothing in the right colour pile. The pink dog gets walked once every recess. I'm proud of this peaceful house. It's a change. I'm the one who painted it at the beginning of the school year. That was my ticket into the girls' circle.

Curious friends come to see us to figure out why we're laughing so much. They're searching for the pink house's secret. If I laugh loudly, it's because I cry just as much. If I laugh loudly, it's so that no one forgets I exist.

I don't know why, but one day, they decide they've had enough of me. They decide that I burned the turkey in the oven.

"A boy in the kitchen, in any case, just isn't possible."

I despise them. My eyes fill with tears. "It's unacceptable; everyone should have a place."

I realize I'm screaming. Students turn around. I'm exiled from the pink house club.

I walk around a bit before the end of recess. I go see the boys. They play at being doctors, mechanics, carpenters, plumbers. They stare at me. I would like to join them, in the way they take their jobs seriously. I dream of theatre stages, shows, songs. I dream of existing under the spotlight. They do adult jobs. I tell myself that I'll have all the time to play at being an adult during the rest of my life.

During the next few recesses, I become friends with a doll, despite what others might think about this boy holding a doll in her hands. I feel like hitting them but I restrain myself. I don't want to reproduce what goes on at home. I rock my doll while telling her to forget the yelling. I have access to a self-fashioned paradise. It's enough to lounge around with her in the light of May as it floods the class in the afternoon.

I ask Martine if I can take the doll with me for summer vacation. She suggests I ask my parents for one for my birthday. I reply dryly, "It's out of the question; it'll make my dad mad." I insist by saying I'll be Pénélope's guardian, and I'll bring my little girl back when school starts again.

"If I let you, all the kids will want to bring toys home…"

It's distressing to think that my little blonde daughter, with her matted hair that I detangle once a week, beautiful from the love I give her, will have to spend all summer alone. I hide her behind the pots and pans of the fake kitchenette so she can be safe from the monsters, from the night, and from the sad ghost prince. I tell her, before leaving, that the holidays will pass quickly and I'll be back soon.

My nights are unbearable, filled with anguish. I have nightmares where she gets stolen or a fire breaks out in the school. I cannot handle the idea of her dying amid the flames.

The last day of school, the bus driver greets me when I get on. "Have a nice summer!"

Radiant like the sun, even on rainy days. He doesn't say it to everyone, so I feel special. When I exit the bus, he gives me a lollipop as a gift for my good behaviour. It's green, lime flavoured, and I know it'll make me wince with happiness. I enter the house excitedly. "Look, Mom, we got lollipops for our good behaviour." Mom isn't there. It makes me sad that there will be no trace of the lollipop left by the time she gets home.

Dad came back recently. He's mowing the lawn before heading back to the North Shore. I want to tell him about my lollipop so he sees that I'm not always stirring up trouble, but he hates being interrupted. He also doesn't like it when we get close to the mower. He's worried we'll end up like the war amputees on TV. "You aren't robots; you don't have interchangeable limbs ike they do. There's a little girl whose leg got mangled because she was running with her dog near the lawn mower and she slipped," he once told me.

I sometimes think about that little girl. The mower haunts me in my nightmares. It follows me. It has my dad's face.

My bed is situated so that the sun floods my face first thing in the morning. I am afraid of the dark. I want to see the sun rise. I stole Pénélope. She's wearing her white dress, unmarked by all of the stories to come that we'll experience together. She didn't fare well during her time in my backpack, so she looks newly dishevelled. I think of Martine, who might have seen me take her and didn't say anything. I think how lucky I am to have this idea in my head and not out in the world. I sit Pénélope on my bed, and introduce her to the morning song orchestrated by the goldfinches and the rustling of the leaves. I tell her that the bed is facing the sun because I'm always afraid it'll be my last night, because I want to be sure that there will still be another day for me. When I'm hurt, Pénélope listens to me. She understands. She wipes my tears. She shows me how to keep my head up. How to handle the darkness. She teaches me that if I stay luminous, I won't have anything to worry about. I hug her tightly when I think of Dad. Next, I apologize for sliding her under my pillow for the day so that my mom doesn't find her, or my dad, or even Olivier. It's necessary.

It's July and Dad has gone back to work. Mom starts going to church more diligently. I have to go with her since there's no one to watch me. The main doors, engraved with angels and saints, open while creaking with age. The saints have accomplished heroic feats, like believing in someone they've never seen.

"If you behave, I'll buy you a chocolate bar after. Now, sit down, and leave a space for Bernard, will you?"

It's hard to believe her, and so I admire the saints even more. Bernard joins us just before the beginning of the service.

I'm wearing a little black jacket with two rows of buttons down the front that makes me look like a little soldier. My beret, on the other hand, makes me look like a French girl. I like my mahogany leather shoes, even though they're too tight. They make me look like a rich girl. I don't walk in them for too long, though, because they make me waddle like a penguin. Mathias is here with his mom. Mathias and the freckles on his cheekbones protruding with laughter. His good mood is contagious.

The people in the choir, in their long, white, angelic gowns, who all look alike, warm up their voices before mass. The smell of incense and myrrh from the previous day still floats in the air and mixes with the woody odour of the benches.

"Why does Jesus bleed on the cross?" Surely he hasn't bled his whole life? Why do we always see him suffering?"

My mom nudges me with her elbow because I shouldn't be asking those kinds of questions; it's blasphemous. "Don't talk about Jesus like that, especially not in his home. He sacrificed himself for us."

My mom closes her eyes again and returns to her praying. I pull at her dress. She looks around to make sure no one can hear my slanderous remarks.

"If I were to sacrifice myself for everyone, I would want it to make them happy and put them in a good mood."

My mom remains silent.

I join Mathias at the back of the room while everyone is praying. I feel like running around. I can no longer hold still. I slide in between him and Rachel. He pulls at my beret. It's hard not to laugh with him. We stifle our laughter with our hands so as to not bother anyone. When everyone has their eyes closed, Bernard gently grabs my mom's hand. Some people sniff, sigh, open their eyes. I can hear whispers of, "I knew it…"

I must at all costs immerse myself in Rachel and Mathias's benevolent warmth. I feel like I'm in a cocoon, for a moment. At least I have them, even though my heart is pounding and I'm filled with fear.

For my first communion, my mom gifts me an illustrated Bible. The images I discover inside are shocking: people with eyes rolled back, white gazes without pupils fixed on the sky. Thieves whose hands have been cut off as punishment for their crimes. The colours are so vibrant that the blood seems like it's about to seep out of the book. I feel like telling them not to worry, that I'll clean their wounds. I think to myself that one day I will also lose my hands because I broke the school window with a rock. I'm worried I will die before my confirmation and then be sent to Hell.

Despite my rollercoaster of emotions, I take curious pleasure in reading the Bible. They're like stories for adults. I underline the passages that fascinate me, like when Jesus walks on water or multiplies the bread. I wonder if I can do the same at home. It would cost us less. Mom starts laughing when I tell her this. I read to Pénélope after supper. I lower my voice, afraid someone might hear me. Otherwise, I read passages to Mathias during recess. He listens to me with a monk's attention. I like seeing the amazement on his face when I give the characters voices.

"It's as though we're actually there!"

One day when a torrential rain falls on the village, I warn him of an impending flood. My mom was right to think that, one day, it would happen. On the weekends, we scour the forest behind Mathias's place to collect large branches. We're trying to build a raft. We take rope that's in his dad's garage to tie the branches together. Week after week, the raft starts to take shape. We are ready for the disaster.

If we're not assembling the raft, we're doing crafts at his house on the living room table. He teaches me origami techniques. I learn how to make airplanes, a swan, and a rabbit with the pages of a Sears catalogue. Even though Mathias praises me, I still think that my animals look more like lousy balls of crumpled paper in comparison to his. A few of his airplanes end their flight in my back. It makes us laugh because I always jump when the tip touches my skin. When taking apart his airplanes, I see hearts drawn on the paper. I think that they're maybe for me but he says, picking his nose, "I'm practising for when I finally send one to Melissa."

My mouth goes dry. I feel myself slipping. I remind myself that Mathias likes girls, and I am not one.

At the mall in town, Mom and I wander through the wings without a specific goal. We need a change of atmosphere. We pass by a dress store. The crinoline makes me daydream. The sequins are no longer on the dress; they're in my eyes. Mom pulls me by the sleeve of my coat, but I stay fixed in front of the shop window.

"Mom, I want a dress. I think it would look nice on me."

"Are you joking? Dresses are for girls."

"So? Melissa has one, you'll see. Everyone compliments her when she wears it."

My mom watches me, waiting for me to finally burst out laughing to let her know it's all a joke and I'm just showing off as usual. But there's no question of it. I remain stationed in front of the window. The store's manager watches me from the other side of her counter. She is cutting up fabric. I enter the store.

"Could you make me a dress ma'am?"

Mom pulls harder and I leap back, out of breath. I follow her reluctantly and then my anger explodes.

"I want the dress!!!"

Everyone is looking at us. My tears fall on their own. Lava rises into my eyes and burns me.

"I want the dress!!!"

"This is the last time you come shopping with me, do you understand?"

My sobs continue in the car. I'm terribly angry that I didn't get a dress. I kick the seat in front of me. I feel like I'm going to disappear from Mathias's life and that thought hurts.

When we get home, I don't take off my shoes. I seize the first object within my reach: the commemorative plate that my grandmother in Québec gave my parents for their tenth anniversary. My mom is in the doorway. I throw it. She moves. She almost gets the plate full in the face.

"Okay, you're going to calm down. You're acting like your father."

She takes me by the arm and leads me to my room. I scream even louder as I struggle. My head whips back suddenly. My mom has slapped me. She seems surprised at herself. My scream stops abruptly. I start crying.

"I hate you!"

I push her out of my room and slam the door. My cheeks tingling, I head to the window. Birds are sleeping on the branch without suspecting that a violence has broken me. They're beautiful, but their beauty doesn't temper my growing turmoil.

My dad leaves for too long again. My mom falls into a depression. She stares at the kitchen wall for many long minutes. She often talks on the phone. When I try to figure out who she's speaking to by entering her room, she briskly responds, "It's none of your business. Go back to your room." She pushes the door with her foot to close it a little more.

Olivier often watches me because my mom doesn't take vacation days. She prefers to be dizzy with work. At the start of the school year I will be asked, same as every year, how my summer went. I'll have to use my imagination. I'll tell my class that my mom taught me the names of the flowers and birds we happened upon during our numerous forest walks; that her voice, tender and muffled, would lull me to sleep for my afternoon naps; that she would kiss me on the forehead while telling me she loved me. I'll tell them that the happy things that don't exist are often more painful than the sad things that do.

We take out a plastic bowl to bake. I bring out the flour, milk, brown sugar. Olivier licks his lips, excited to make his favourite meal, crepes. We put on some music. Joe Dassin returns to warm the house. I feel independent, staying home alone like this with Olivier. He mixes the ingredients. I go grab the cinnamon, like Mom likes. I pour the milk in small doses as my brother mixes vigorously, so as not to leave any lumps. We start dancing during "Le petit pain au chocolat." Olivier spins me around until the smell of burning breaks us out of our trance. In our euphoria, we foolishly left the stove unattended. Fire erupts out of the dishcloth left too close to the element and the flame is already large. Panicked, Olivier starts running all over the house trying to find something to put it out with. The flame dances with fervour. It brushes the stove hood. I stay passive. I don't even bat an eyelash. I watch Olivier run himself dizzy. I don't know why I don't feel like moving, I just know that the fire is calling to me and we speak the same language. Olivier musters up his courage, takes the situation into his own hands, grabs the cloth, and throws it into the sink. The fire doesn't disappear. It devours the window. It even looks like it's eating the faraway apple trees. It wriggles to engulf everything I want it to.

"Why aren't you helping me?" Olivier screeches at me, in panic. "Come on, move!"

It's like I no longer know how to speak.

"Help me! We're going to burn!"

I regain my senses and throw him a bag of flour within my reach. He dumps the contents over it in one go, which immediately extinguishes the fire. Another couple of seconds and the fire would have gotten to the curtains. We hurry to hide the marks of our carelessness. A bit later, Olivier returns to the crepe mix.

"So, Mom is going to be happy, eh?" Olivier says with his big Cheshire Cat smile.

He's proud of his success. Olivier is making his fourth crepe when Mom gets home.

It's the first time that Olivier and I go to summer camp. Dad is away for part of the summer and Mom is pulling doubles. Anxiety cramps my stomach. I have to go to the bathroom several times, praying it'll go away. My stomach lets out gurgles that sound like wolves howling on the night of a full moon.

"Mom, I have a wolf in my stomach."

It makes her laugh, takes her out of her unstable spells. I'm often met with a porcelain face, eyes as empty as an abandoned shell. With my mom, I start to bury my imagination away in the deepest silence.

The camp is situated in the middle of a forest. When we arrive, we can see a small cabin amid the pine, ash, and birch trees. This place tremors with poetic beauty. Many small buildings are set side by side to form a half circle. There's also a dorm where dreams are made. We'll sleep there sometimes; it's part of the summer plan. Enormous columns of pruned cedar border the campgrounds. I'll have to cross these lines as well. François, the camp counsellor, must be seventeen. It's his summer job, watching small turbulent monsters. He comes out of the main building when our car parks at the grey-blue gravel entrance. He has a scar on his upper lip. It makes him look tough. Already, I picture him as a pirate scouring the ocean; already, he is glorious to me. A bunch of kids are having fun in the grass, and they are small dandelions filled with laughter. No one is crying here; you could say it's paradise.

I want François to tell me about his past as a pirate and all his adventures at sea. A laughing mouth peeks through his growing beard. He opens my car door and it's all that's needed to win me over. The anxiety that had been nagging at me since the morning dissipates. It's as though, with one look, he tamed the wolf in my stomach.

I take my time stepping out of the car, and the ease with which I move is like snow melting in an unexpected spring, which laughs on in amusement. My hand is in his so I don't fall. Another quarter of a second to cherish, another reminder that I'm alive. I set my feet on the gravel. As for Olivier, he looks like a horse that's been let out of its paddock onto the racetrack.

François has just come back from a game of golf. His beige shorts are rolled at the bottom and reveal his powerful, muscular thighs. His white tank top shows off his hot arms, dripping with sweat. I don't know how to deal with his effect on me. I become all red and I blame the summer heat, not my hunger for love. He looks at me with fresh eyes, lush Amazon-forest eyes, eyes you could get lost in without fear. I take pleasure in the attention he gives me. I understand, in his gaze, that I exist because of others; if I'm not seen, I don't exist. Olivier hides under the cedar hedges and asks me to come play.

Mom gets back in the car. "Be safe. Make sure that they're careful, those two monkeys!" she says to the camp counsellor, who gives her a reassuring wave.

The car pulls away, whirring. It's the first time Mom has left me on my own, and I'm so worked up. Finally, I can be alone with François. I feel like she could have overshadowed me, my umbrella mother.

The sun starts to beat down on us and the smell of citronella wafts through the air, keeping the mosquitoes away. They show us around. In the dorms, boys and girls are separated, but all the activities are in mixed teams. There's a kitchen where a woman and a man are busy cooking nourishing dishes that will give us energy during busy days. The main room has chairs like at school, benches and cushions all over the ground, and a round table that allows us to meet as a group. I don't want to be in the cabin of boyish farting and belching, but I don't say anything. I don't want to draw attention to myself.

We're welcomed with fresh lemonade. Other parents drop off their children in the meantime. We're under a little canopy set up for the occasion. There are balloons of every colour and banners with flowers drawn on them. Yellow sweat stains form around the armpits of François's tank top and, when he passes close to me, I breathe in his salty, wild smell. He greets the parents who leave their kids in his care. He tucks his blond curls behind his ears. The slogan "Here, We Grow" is printed on his baseball cap in neon yellow. That's it, I'm a bud waiting to flower. I hope it will happen quickly. I don't understand this sudden urge to carry life in my stomach, both because I'm so young and I also don't have the physical setup for giving birth. I find it fun that I'm able to be whomever I want in my fantasies.

It's clear that when I get home, I'll talk about this man in the multicoloured pages of my diary. He'll be the first in a procession of romances:

Today, he put me on his shoulders and I became a living tower. I felt my heart beat between my thighs.

Nadine, the other camp counsellor, talks to him often. I don't have the courage to tell her not to get too close to my pirate. She cut me off, once. Why doesn't she just content herself with cutting flowers at the edge of the forest instead?

I put some crushed raspberries on my lips; it is like pretty red lipstick. I hope I'll be able to leave a sugary trace on one of his cheeks at some point.

I wrap each description of him with love, every moment we spend together. In the bucolic splendour of the summer camp, I have my first erection.

The days at camp pass at lightning speed, so much so that when they come close to ending, I pout in disgust. Disgust at having to go back home into that strange atmosphere. I can't quite stomach that my mom sometimes gets rid of us so that she can go to the beach with her friends and Bernard. I know because once, when she wasn't working, there were beach towels and a blow-up ball in the trunk, and sandals that weren't hers.

There's no clock at camp. We rely on the sun to know which activities it's time to do. It's time for crafts in the early afternoon, it's time for playing in the sandbox, it's time to go on the water slide.

My favourite moment of the day is when we work on our herbarium project, which we're trying to finish it by the end of our stay. I gorge myself on the present offered to me: the sounds of rustling leaves sound like waterfalls, the chirping of the furtive goldfinches falls silent as we pass, the green promise of a smiling summer stirs me, the cicadas' concert enchants me, the plant shadows glide over the tall blond grass. I'm this forest that we inhabit entirely, that we hope is made wild by life.

The field is dotted with bright yellow splashes of dandelions that make me think of stars in a green sky. It's a shame that people have the tendency to mow them. Here, there is no question of them being removed. It's probably the first time that I've seen such big ones. Nothing natural is removed here.

The camp counsellor bends down to my level. "We have to let them grow. When they become adults, their heads get white, and if we blow on them, their hair flies away. That way, they live a second life."

It's enough, later in the season, to watch them float like jellyfish, to appreciate the soft happy slowness of existence. A summer of beauty is orchestrated before my eyes, filling me with bliss I have never known. My soul is happy. In love.

Once, when I'm alone with François, we cut up cardboard to write down the names of the plant species found during our expeditions. I sneak a few furtive glances in my pirate's direction. He has the charming habit of squeezing his tongue between his lips when he's concentrating.

"What's making you laugh?"

"Nothing, nothing!"

He laughs.

Olivier becomes friends with some of the bad kids. It runs in the family. When it's too calm, it's absolutely necessary to find trouble. He climbs trees and throws pinecones and small branches to his friends. It's a time when a war can break out as quickly as peace is restored over lemonade. I draw a lot. I like finding myself in front of a piece of paper. I draw the new flowers that I discover.

The only moment I dread is when we do water sports. Everyone goes in shouting their enthusiasm, but I feel like shutting them up. How can they find pleasure in getting undressed in front of others, parading naked, their chests out there for everyone to see? It's a punishment. I am jealous of their joy. I cover my chest and it makes the others laugh. Once, unbeknownst to her, I saw a girl's privates while she was changing near the shed. I wondered why I didn't have one like her. François brings me a shirt so I can rejoin the group. "For a little boy, you're pretty shy…" He gives me a little tap on the head and encourages me to enjoy the nice weather and the small lake on the edge of the camp.

In the evening, I ask my mom why I don't have a thin line like the girl I saw earlier. "We call that a vulva and it's because you're a boy. Boys have penises. Girls have vulvas."

Her response doesn't erase the uneasiness that I feel about what I have between my legs and what I don't.

During one of our expeditions to improve the herbarium, I make sure to be the first to ask questions, to point at every new plant or flower that we discover. I want to be sure that François pays attention to me. When he's close, I enjoy the woody smell of his tanned and musky skin, it makes me dazed and I feel it in the pit of my stomach. Sometimes Nadine is the one to respond and that annoys me. I nod my head but I don't listen. I start hating her more every day, imagining her catching fire under the weight of my gaze. When she gets close to him, my heart tightens, like a mandarin clenched in my fingers when I'm angry. I am on the verge of exploding. I watch the way she sways her hips and mimic her in the evenings, imagining François hypnotized by the swing of mine. She leads the craft classes. She always puts her long hair into two braids, one on each side. Her upturned nose makes her look like a pig. I despise her as best I can. It worries me that she might be going out with François. Sometimes, they hug and I feel like I've disappeared. I think about taking a saw to her high lifeguard chair, just one leg. I think one day it'll work; she'll fall off as soon as she sits down. A bamboo branch destroyed by jealousy. Oh, it's so fun to think about. I find a small saw in the workbench that's always left unlocked. It's wonderful to be so inconspicuous. Sometimes, when no one is looking, I start to saw a leg. I hide the saw under a large rock near the lake. No one sees me. I think about lighting her dorm on fire, but the saw is more accessible than a match. When she gets what she deserves, I'll once again find beauty in the sky.

One day, François gives me a small bouquet of wildflowers that grow in the forest as a present. "These are yarrow."

I contemplate the white arrangement in my hands. It's like he just gave me a wedding bouquet. I wonder why I deserve this attention. Little blue flowers are sprinkled within the offering. I ask him. "Why these?"

"Because it reminds me of the colour of your eyes and since I can't put the sky in a bouquet, I thought these small flowers would make you happy."

In this moment, I don't know that this bouquet will grow with me and even survive from apartment to apartment, through all my future moves. I'll think about these flowers during every breakup. If I love these flowers too much, they will dry and disintegrate in my hands. It is the flowering of my passions, and in the deepest recesses of my heart, I already know that I will never escape them. That this camp will live with me forever; it will fill me with tenderness when I think about it later, as a grown-up. François talks to me all summer about the flowers with such enthusiasm, I no longer know who or what I'm in love with. Because it's ambiguous, I decide to be in love with everything. The trees, the grass, his eyes, his mouth that I want on my cheek, or maybe even on my lips.

Another swim in the lake. Many rocks are scattered around. It's an artificial lake that was dug up when the camp was founded. Nadine's high chair is there and it's been a while since I've had an opportunity to saw the leg. It's like the bouquet assuaged me. When Nadine's perched on top, she looks like she's on a throne, regal, reigning over her small subjects and her kingdom. She's always in her lavender bathing suit that hugs her late-adolescent curves. I dream of having her hips. She has all of François's attention and she doesn't have to question it. Some of the younger kids do pirouettes near the water. They jump on a platform installed in the guise of a trampoline before disappearing under the water, a bit muddy, and come back out making sea monster noises. I'm wearing the white shirt François gave me to swim in. I'm still terrified of being shirtless like the other boys.

"You look like a ghost. You're just as white as your shirt," one of the boys from another village tells me.

"Don't listen to them. They have nothing better to do," Olivier comforts me.

I can't help it; I clench my jaw and my fists. In this humid summer afternoon, Nadine leaves her throne to go smoke.

I decide to go into the water, not too deep, just up to my knees. It's refreshing but it's not the river. I miss it and my mom who watches us doing acrobatics.

Three kids gather around me and block my way. They try to catch me. I try in vain to escape. They grab hold of one of my legs, then the other, and make me fall into the water. They try to get a hold of my shirt. I resist as much as I can. I'm fighting an octopus. One of them pulls on my leg, another turns me face down in the water. I get frightened and struggle to my feet. He pulls again and I smash my tailbone on a rock. I don't understand why they're laughing. One boy grabs me by the neck and presses with enough strength to block my airway. Faced with their curious looks, I go from ghost to red flag in a fraction of a second and they're goading me on in their bullfight.

My vision starts to fog. One of them throws chunks of mud. I scream. I look for Nadine. They throw me in the water. They hold me by the feet as I thrash and try to stay above water. I don't even know if I actually want to stay alive to confront their curious faces, huddled together in amazement.

A jolt of lightning rips through my stomach.
Flowers rot on the boiling summer asphalt.
Mom closes the car door.
They grab the throat of a swan and deprive it of its song.
Dad's fist breaks its bones.
It's a table that breaks.
I no longer understand.

They try to take my shirt off. It comes off in one go, like a layer of skin burned by the sun. They try to take my

[88]

shorts off. They don't succeed but they still manage to pull them down to my knees. The others can see my privates and my butt. I try to hide myself with my hands. A hand takes a hold of mine. I'm saved from the definitive silence. They take me out of the water. I pull my shorts up as best I can. It's Olivier. He came to save me. He screams, "Shut up!" and shoves the boys out of our way.

François arrives in a panic. I'm ashamed to have him see me like this. Nadine comes back from her smoke. He berates her for not being there and for having allowed this violence to happen in her absence. I gradually come to my senses. My brother covers me with a towel. His embrace is soft. I cough out the water in my lungs. Olivier takes me in his arms. Seeing that François doesn't soften his anger towards Nadine's negligence and that she seems to shrink on the spot, I smile over Olivier's shoulder.

The weeks proceed in their colourful parade. I grow, with strange recurring sensations in the pit of my stomach. This desire pushes me to put a pillow in between my legs at bedtime, as if to snuff it out at its origin. I grind my hips and think often about François. My eyes roll back in satisfaction. The body, unbeknownst to others, finds its own words.

M om has asked Dad to call us at least once a week. His hoarse voice stresses me out. I've never noticed the fatigue in my dad's voice. I thought he was immune to it.

"Did you catch a cold in the woods?"

"Who gets sick in the middle of summer? No, we're just doing long shifts, that's all."

I would like for him to tell me that he misses us, that he can't wait to play outside with me, that he can't wait to see Mom.

I dreamed of Dad and I didn't feel like jumping into his arms.

Bernard comes to mow the lawn and Mom still makes him pies. He waves from the window but my hand is too weighed down by my dad's absence to respond to him. His hello hits the window like a stunned bird.

I was really sad today because I thought about that time at the lake and I'm afraid of being under the covers. It reminds me of the water above my head. Bernard said he would take care of me. Today, I sat on his legs and he pretended to be a horse. Clip-clop, clip-clop. I bounced up and down on his thighs. It was like I had the hiccups but they weren't coming from my body. I told him to take me far. He thought that was weird. Horses are for going to far-off places, right? Maybe this way, I could go on an adventure. He gives Mom a lot of kisses.

It's a languid summer. Mathias is off vacationing in Maine with his parents so I have to play outside alone most of the time. I'm a spy or the girl boss of an elf army. The trees serve as soldiers under my governance. They stand straight, waiting for my orders. I'm the first female army commander-in-chief, the first in the history of the world. My superpowers allow me to defend myself. Sometimes, when I'm really angry, balls of fire burst from my palms and I burn fields of stubborn soldiers to a crisp. Other times, I'm Princess Amidala from *Star Wars* and I fall in love with Obi-Wan Kenobi.

Sometimes, Olivier joins me.

"I'm going to be Hercules and you'll be Achilles. Together we'll conquer the world."

I tell him that I would prefer to be Megara. I discovered her character in the Hercules cartoon on TV before heading to school. The hero falls in love with Megara at first sight.

Olivier isn't bothered and he's even impressed. He finds that I convincingly embody my female character. When we lay under the tree, always in our game, I put my head on his chest and let myself be lulled by the movements of his breath. I'm still embodying a character. A whole summer spent being someone else.

When our game turns sour, my brother says, "You're

way too dramatic! You're too distressed. It's no fun playing with you."

I'm damned to keep playing Megara. I go into the house to pout. I fill in the pages of my journal.

Today, Olivier didn't want me to play the girlfriend. He asked me to play a commander in Achilles's army and I didn't want to. I still wanted to play Megara and we fought.

I float when I am on Hercules's chest.

If Olivier wasn't my brother, I think I would be in love with him.

The wind rustles the leaves. Sometimes I fall asleep in the tall grass beneath the August sun.

Sometimes. I hide so well in the middle of the woods that it takes Olivier almost an hour to find me. I laugh, hidden in the branches, not making a sound. The birds coo in the balsam fir trees, their little heads bobbing when they see Olivier. They're more afraid than I am. I don't move from my hiding spot even though he's visibly exasperated. I leave the woods with the sticky scent of spruce and pine in my hair. I rarely shower at night. I bring the forest to my pillow to guarantee a peaceful sleep. I think of the moments when I sink my fingers into the hundred-year-old lichen. I think of the heart that I still don't understand. I think that if I sank my fingers into it, it would feel like this vegetal moss. When Hades succeeds in finding me, I am condemned to Hell. I accept my fate. Being carried away by the current is all I know.

I'm at the beach with Mom and Bernard. He has come to join us. He brought buckets and small shovels made of plastic to help build our castles. Mom serves us lemonade in her two-piece cherry-patterned white bathing suit. She put her hair up in an enormous chignon that looks like a beehive. Mom is queen of the bees. Dad comes back from work when we are hollowing out a path for the lake in the sand. He notices Bernard. They're like two dogs that can't smell each other. My dad's body tenses up. Bernard goes to meet him. The two face each other like in a western. We hear a bark. We can't tell what they're saying. It all stays contained in a hand gesture motioning towards the opposite end of the beach. Mom gets involved. Bernard leaves without looking back. It looks like my dad has come back from the war. He's gotten thinner. White hairs in his jet-black beard. He drops his bag and gets on his knees to play with Olivier and me in the sand. Mom gives him a glass of lemonade. They kiss so that their lips barely touch. They never explain to us what's going on. I notice that they've both lost a lot of weight. My parents are going to disappear in front of our eyes.

At home, my mom is withdrawn as she clears the table. Dad tries to make conversation with us, but we see each other so rarely that our responses are as short as his absences are long.

"Hey, you. What do you say we go out and pick blueberries?"

Even though I don't find the offer exciting, I don't hesitate, not even for a second, before saying yes. The smile on his face and the light in his eyes are rare. He's wearing his quilted hunting jacket, even though it's the middle of summer. I get used to the smell of gasoline that emanates from him because he works with power saws and chainsaws. Later, I will become a fan of *The Texas Chainsaw Massacre*, not because of the horror, but because the sound of the chainsaw will remind me of the music my dad created all summer. No one ever asks us to describe our parents' smell. I would say that my dad smells like gasoline and that he emanates a sense of distance.

In his truck, a Madonna song crackles through the old speakers. I lip-synch and mimic dramatic diva moves. I want to put on a good show for him.

The road is bumpy and the white leather upholstery, heated by the sun, burns my thighs. I don't care. For one rare moment, I'm with my dad. It's a special occasion. Solar bliss. The swelling of our lungs. Love blooming.

On the way to the lake taking the 138, I lower my window and stick my head out of the car. At the same time, I bring out my summer smile. I feel like shouting to the world that my dad is finally back home.

In my excitement, I lose my hat to the wind. It ends its journey in a ditch. "Put your head back inside now. We're going to look for your hat."

"No, it's okay, it would be fun to see a hat tree growing next year."

He changes the station on the radio, Led Zeppelin now playing.

In the clearing, the scent of the black spruce intoxicates me. Dandelion fluff floats in the laziness of the heat wave. I think about François who told me that dandelions have two lives. It's beautiful to watch them start their second lives. They seem better like this: light, carefree, liberated from gravity.

Buckets in our hands, I let my dad lead the way. I never noticed before how large his shoulders are, nor the big paws that serve as his hands. I understand why my mom shrinks away when he wants to hit her.

He's handsome, my dad, standing in the middle of the field. His brown eyes look at me from time to time to make sure I'm still there. At his side, I feel like nothing bad could happen to us. I'm sure he would beat a bear with his bare hands. I think I see a tear in the corner of his eye. I think that it makes him look so beautiful.

"Why are you crying, Dad?"

"The light is blinding me. The sun is strong. I forgot my sunglasses... Come on... we have tons of blueberries to pick here."

Determined to fill my bucket faster than him, I drift, elated, from grove to grove. It's impossible to stop. As the gymnastics of my picking gets better and better, I think I could qualify for the Olympics if it one day became a competitive sport.

Dad tries to help me reach the blueberries that are out of my reach but he loses his footing, spills all the contents of his bucket—which flips in the air—and does a somersault. Unexpectedly, he laughs and I laugh in turn. It lasts several minutes. It could have lasted an eternity. It feels funny to hear us laughing together. I search my memory in vain for the last time that it happened.

When we put the buckets overflowing with blueberries into the car, the sun starts to hide behind the mountains and gives the clouds a burnt orange hue. My dad searches for something in the truck. He comes out with a gun in his hands, a 12-gauge.

"You'll see, my boy, real men fire guns. They hunt. Take a good look."

My stomach is on fire.

He raises the rifle, rests it on his shoulder, and heads towards the woods. He fires. The blast is striking. I feel like my soul is going to leave my body. My ears hurt. I stiffen. A few birds fly away, crying out in surprise.

He hands me the gun so I can take my turn firing it. It's heavy. I can hardly hold it up straight. "You're going to shoot yourself in the foot, my boy, if you stay like that. Lift it back up right away, come on."

The sun keeps setting.

"Dad, we have to go back. It's late. Mom will be worried."

I look for an excuse so I don't have to shoot. I can't find one.

"Not until you've shot the gun, my boy. Look, aim at the tree trunk there."

I close one eye like he just did. I pull the trigger. My love for my dad disappears as quickly as the bullet. The strength of the blow almost dislocates my shoulder. The bullet disappears somewhere in the woods. I hear a ricochet followed by the rustling of leaves. I have tinnitus for five whole minutes.

"I didn't like that," I tell him, letting the gun fall to the ground. I cry. I get in the car. Fasten my seatbelt. I'm ready to go.

"Son, you're a real wimp. Get a grip on yourself. I didn't raise a faggot."

We return home. The lightness I felt this afternoon is replaced by the leaden weight of my disenchantment. I sink deep into my seat and don't hear him talking. I save the rest of my tears for my bedroom. It hurts. It's more painful than holding in a full bladder. I'm still in shock from the gunfire. I stare at the glove compartment, transfixed by the memory of the gun in my hand. It's the first time that, in the car, I didn't look out at the passing landscape.

Back home, I tell Mom that Dad taught me how to shoot a gun. Another fight storms through the house. I should have kept my mouth shut.

We have a test in music class. We have to play the recorder. I've been practising to play "Au clair de la lune" for two weeks, enough to drive Olivier crazy. He threatens to send me to play on the moon so that I'll leave him alone. I hate the humidity that forms in the tube when we play and, when we play for too long, the smell of foul breath.

The teacher has long nails—to play the guitar. I idolize this man who feminizes his fingers. I'd like to muster up enough courage to do it too. Each student presents their recorder piece. Some have to play the same song as me, others have to play "À la claire fontaine" or "Meunier, tu dors." As I get ready to start my evaluation and my lips press tightly against the mouthpiece of the instrument, someone knocks on the door. The teacher asks me to follow him. A woman stands in the doorway.

"Hello, I'm Fabienne. I work for the Director of Youth Protection. Your dad isn't doing too well. He needs some rest," she tells me.

I glance at the class behind me. Mathias looks back questioningly. I shrug my shoulders. They lead me out to a car. I decide to stop following them and run away. They only just manage to grab me. I can't run. During the drive, we pass by roads I don't know. They take me to the department where families are broken apart.

"Your mom and dad fought this afternoon. Some neighbours called the police." That's why I'm here. "You're in good hands."

Fabienne turns to me and throws me a smile that I don't catch.

I panic. I don't know where my mom is, nor my brother. No one seems to want to tell me. I try to contain the anxiety that coats my stomach and my heart. Nervousness makes me crack my joints. I pinch my thighs to distract myself from the pain.

When we get to the office, I sit at a long rectangular table, and Fabienne, a file in hand, sits all the way at the end. They give me a glass of water that I won't drink. I become tiny in this chair. I'm asked all sorts of questions about my dad. They ask if he's touched this or that part of my body, how he acts with other children, with my mom. "Is it the first time that your parents have fought?"

Reluctantly, I respond "no." It burns my mouth to tell them about the time Olivier had blood on his face. I notice my mom in the hallway through the blinds on the window. She paces back and forth. During my interview with Fabienne, she sits, gets back up, goes outside for a smoke.

Measures are being taken.

My mom says, "You and Olivier will go stay with my cousin, just until everything gets sorted out."

I return to the car, my mom's this time. Olivier sits beside me.

"Mom, you can't do this to us, Mom…" I can't control my sobs.

"I don't have a choice."

In the rear-view mirror, I can see the streaks of mascara on my mom's cheeks.

In my journal, I write:

A woman came to school and, as though she had lightning in her hands, she destroyed everything in her way.

The evening we leave for Manon's, my mom's cousin, we prepare a little box of personal effects. I bring the porcelain statuettes that my mom buys me every time we're in town. Their playful expressions might do me some good. I might feel less alone. It's a moonless night.

It's so dark. It's like molasses has been spilled onto the house.

Mom has just stuck the last strip of Scotch Tape onto the box filled with my souvenirs when a tear falls down my cheek. She pushes the box with a kick of her foot, grumbling in exasperation. Olivier then brings it to the car. We're going to Manon's, who we almost never talk to, except during the holidays. It was this or a foster family, and my brother and I would have been separated, on top of everything else.

I take a last look around the house. The echo of my footsteps is a goodbye I don't want to hear. I look at the corridors where I've cried, where I've hidden from my brother with mounting excitement at the idea of being found. I hope with all my heart that I forgot something so that I can go back to my room. I think about Mathias on the edge of my bed, showing me how to fold paper airplanes with hearts not meant for me. These planes no longer jab at my back. I don't know how long I'll stay there but, in my child's mind, I'm going away for life. Before hopping into the car, I clench my teeth, my fists, my memories.

We pass by the school. I no longer see it the same way, not with the same eyes or the same heart. From now on, it will be synonymous with the dismantling of my family. And the recorder lesson when everything was turned upside down will haunt me for years.

Manon greets us with open arms in her white and blue two-storey home. She takes our luggage and gives us a kiss. We are lucky that she has always liked us. At Christmas parties, she is the person who spoils us with the most presents. She has always liked us because she can no longer have children, ever since her car accident. Happily, before that, she had Michelle, who's now in high school.

Manon catches up with my mom, and Olivier and I explore the house. All of the bedrooms are upstairs and a stairway painted pink leads us there. A room is reserved for us. For the first time, I'll share a room with my brother. We'll sleep in the same bed. There's a large, half-empty bookshelf where we can put our stuff. Mom and Manon have been talking for about ten minutes. My mom bursts into tears on her cousin's shoulder, and Manon wraps her tightly in her arms. It's not going to be fun. She leaves and waves bye from her car window; she's going back to war.

During our stay, Mom calls two or three times a week to make sure everything is going alright. I start reading during our stay. There's a bookshelf filled to the brim with Kundera, Sartre. I don't understand a lot of what I read in those books at that age, but I discover a ferocious interest in reading. A chance to muffle the voices in my head with theirs.

The war between my mom and dad lasts several weeks. Now when she arrives, her face is sad. "Your father and I are going to get a divorce."

I deal with the shock by throwing myself on the couch. Olivier and I wrap ourselves in each other's arms, and Mom joins us, covering us with her perforated wings.

Manon works at the bank. She comes home with a sigh that sounds like trucks groaning down the coast. I don't talk to her right away because I'm worried I'll bother her. I go back to playing with my horse figurines. Time goes by faster than at my parents' house because she often talks to us. She puts in her rollers once or twice weekly to get meticulously placed brown curls for work. She does this with military precision. Everything has to be exact, nothing should stick out.

Coming back from work, she tosses her shoes in the entrance before sitting in her rocking chair for a minute. I give her a little show with my bizarre horse races. She has the blissful look of someone on holiday when she watches me play. Her smile brightens the living room. Manon is luminous; she is the island in the middle of a storm. She's not afraid of offending me or talking to me about what's going on.

"I'm worried that Mom and Dad will never see each other again."

"It'll happen, kiddo. You have to be aware of that, just like it's possible that they get back together at some point. But with time, you'll see, everything happens for good reason."

I start to cry. I don't know if it's because of the end

of the storm or if it's because, for the first time, I'm being told what's actually going on.

She stretches her arms out for a hug. I bury my head between her neck and her thick brown hair. I delight in this fragrant humidity. The fruity refined scent of Poison by Dior assails and overwhelms me. Her perfume makes everyone but me sneeze. On the contrary, I take in big whiffs. For me, it's synonymous with calm. It's my walk in the garden. As long as I can smell this perfume, I'm safe. Manon takes a sip of her soft drink. *Pssssscccchhhhhttttt.* The sound that announces that supper is soon.

I put away my horses and we spend the rest of the day on the porch that gives onto the 138. The trucks pass by at an alarming speed. I often imagine myself being crushed while trying to cross the highway. The idea makes me shudder with vertigo. It's why I never play outside. I find the highway too enticing.

The dust swirls in the amber light. Michelle arrives with her friends. Manon leaves the house for a second. Michelle, all curves, ties her hair up in a bun—long brown hair with red highlights—and shows off her bathing suit. She barely notices me. Her friends follow her into the pool. They enter it like I would like to enter the world, with carefree enthusiasm. Manon returns with pressed juice. I listen to the tinkling of ice. The sweat on the glasses condenses and drips onto the small wooden table. I take a gulp. It calms me.

The paint on the porch is peeling. I pick off several pieces of old colour with my fingers. It's a bad habit and Manon taps me gently on the fingers while smiling. The house is situated on a mountainside and the sun glides over the expanse of lichen. The air is humid. I say goodnight to the sun. The shade on the front steps reaches our knees. It's a sign that it's time to go in and start preparing supper. I help by chopping vegetables, stirring the soup or the stew. I take several glances outside to enjoy the last light of the day. The night terrifies me.

There's a stray dog, a mix between a Golden Retriever and a Labrador, that sometimes passes by in the woods at the edge of the yard. He always pants as though he's back from a long journey. His fur, which must have been creamy white at some point, is stained with oil or mud. I talk to him. We're not allowed to feed him or pet him because he might have fleas. I don't care about that. He's so skinny you can see his ribs, just like me. As long as he and I keep meeting on the porch after supper, it's a continued sign that we're both committed to no longer disappearing.

My nighttime worries cause me to imagine trouble. It seems like the trees are closing in on the house and choking it. The sunsets accumulate but the sky remains full of anguish. Always this threatening sky that I keep hoping to evade.

I have my first taste of alcohol during this stay. There are bottles in the kitchen above the china cabinet. When Charles, Manon's husband, is busy in the henhouse, I climb a small stool to reach them. Unsteady, I stretch my legs and tiptoeing, pull myself up, hoping no one sees the little kid trying to taste her first sip. With my fingertips, I manage to move a bottle forward, then rush to unscrew the cap. I smell the aromas: a dry note that makes me crinkle my nose and burns my nostrils when I inhale it. I drink a thick liquid the texture of maple syrup, with accents of thyme and rosemary. I take in as much as I can before I get caught. It makes me cringe. It stings the inside of my mouth. The alcohol traces an inflamed path in my esophagus. The sensation delights me. It feels like it's disinfecting my insides. All my injuries. I try some more. And more. I drop the bottle. Then rush to pick up the mess. I then return, incognito, to my childish occupations. I cross my fingers that no one will notice that there's a bottle missing.

Charles works in the mines. Passionate about rocks since he was little, he shows me his collection of precious and semi-precious gemstones. On a glass shelf, each piece has its own beam of light to make it shine and enhance its value. An amethyst effloresces in varieties of purple from each of its points; citrine illuminates us with golden warmth; and there is this rose quartz that fascinates me more than anything else, its vibrant pink connecting a matrix of concretions. I ask him if I can hold it in my hands.

"Yes, it's Manon's gem. I gave it to her for our anniversary. There's a lot of femininity emanating from this rock. Grace as well."

I feel good as soon as I hold the gemstone. I have a feeling that a conversation is happening between the stone and me, that it knows something I don't. I feel my heartbeat in my hand or maybe it's the gem's or maybe they're beating in unison. I open my eyes wide and Charles seems amused by my amazement. I ask him if I can borrow it, to sleep with it. He lets me. Strangely, when I clutch the rock tightly before sleeping, my crying fits are shorter. I caress it with my fingertip. I have never been so drawn in by something. The stone sits in my palm as much as possible.

Charles crashes in front of the television and watches his TV shows for the rest of the evening. Most of the time I only see his bald head. A skull with a crown of hair. A blue cloud hovers over his head. He always wears that faded shirt. He always laughs at game-show jokes.

He offers us cookies. He has different ones each week. I close my eyes so I can be surprised by the flavours. I throw myself wholeheartedly into the box. I don't mind that I will have trouble sleeping because of the sugar. I like to stay awake at night to discover the music of this dream house. I open the French doors just a little to let in the murmur of the wooded wilderness. I hope that the mutt will come back to see me. Maybe he will recognize me by my smell.

Manon, during this time, tells me stories from when she and my mom used to see each other weekly during their childhood. They were always a little bit in competition with each other. "Your mother was the bigger daredevil, she was always climbing everything. One time, she climbed the neighbour's fence to go see her little boyfriend at the time. She fell butt first into the mud. You should have seen her stunned face and her fearful expression."

I know a little more about who I take after. It's funny to learn things about my mom from someone else.

"One time at church, your mother accidentally sat on the catechism book, the ones used to follow the ceremony, and when she noticed, she said that she had laid it, and since then, we've called her our little chicken. Your grandmother couldn't stop laughing, so much so that all three of us had to leave the church."

They're good together, Charles and Manon. The gymnastics of their love is enviable. There don't seem to be any storms in their home. I watch them sometimes from the corner of my eye when they kiss and, sometimes, I replace their faces with my parents'. This way, I tell myself that it's not entirely ruined. They plunge into each other's eyes, underwater. Their dance is masterful. It seems to me that whenever my parents try to dance together, they end up treading on each other's feet.

Manon heads to her bedroom after suppertime. She performs her nightly ritual. She takes off her earrings, her rings, and her bracelets. She's like a Christmas tree, her ornaments taken down after the holidays. She puts everything away with great care in her small cherry wood chest. My eyes widen when I look at the jewellery box. I watch from the doorway as she finishes up and turns her attention elsewhere.

I think about all the times I can be alone with it. It has a kind of sacred aura about it, like the chalice in church. This chest holds more than just jewellery; it doesn't just contain my aunt's day but also magical weapons to channel femininity. She wears freshwater pearls during her workdays at the bank and extravagant earrings that look like inverted candlesticks on the weekend. Michelle borrows some of her mother's earrings before going out. I too want to have access to the jewellery case without having to ask permission.

When Manon takes off her makeup in the bathroom, I know I have a few minutes. It's the perfect moment to run into her bedroom. The chest is there, always in the same spot, right in the middle of the dresser, under the feeble glow of the bedside lamp. I have to rush. I make my way through the pile of laundry on the floor.

When I get close, I take the time to admire it once more. Manon always buys herself new jewellery; it's her hobby, so it's always a surprise, just like with the cookies. I glide my fingers softly over the grooves in the wood, as if touching the cheek of a child you don't want to wake. One of the grooves leads me to the always-unlocked latch. A simple press of the finger and I hear a click. I bite my lower lip. My classmates would be this mesmerized by an ice-cream cone; for me, it's these jewels. I see sapphire and ruby rings, emerald necklaces, jade bracelets, citrine earrings... It's joy in crystal form, a real treasure chest. I revel in their presence against my palms, between my fingers. I decide to slip a bracelet or two into my pants pocket. I lip-synch in front of my bedroom mirror, wrapped in sheets made to look like a dress, and a tight scarf on my head that falls down my back, mimicking long hair that I swish to my heart's content. The jewels ornament my body, releasing me from the weight of being a boy.

One time, when I think I am alone, I wear a long pearl necklace around my neck and start dancing. When I do a turn, Manon is in the doorway. I'm stunned. I don't know what to do.

"You know, if you want to wear jewellery, you're welcome to, but ask me next time please."

We both smile.

Mom comes over to celebrate her birthday with us. I am anything but festive. A black forest cake trembles in her hands. When she approaches me, I notice that her eyebrow is twitching with fatigue. Something feels forced. It feels like she doesn't want to be with us.

Two sparklers adorn the cake. The festiveness of the sparklers contrasts against the mournful look on my mom's face. She has a slightly yellowed white dress on. In front of the candles, she looks at us all. She bursts into tears. "This is the first time I'm blowing out the candles without him…"

Manon takes her by the shoulders. "You'll get through it. I'm here. Your kids are here too."

Mom wipes her tears. She concentrates on making a wish. She blows out her candles and smiles. She's just turned thirty. She eats a piece of cake quickly, jokes with us. Since Dad's leaving, it seems like Mom is getting closer to Olivier and me. I remember his laugh in the blueberry fields. I miss my dad fiercely.

It is very frustrating to feel helpless when she seems, despite her joy, to want to explode. In a voice shaky with fear, I ask, "Are we going to go home soon?"

I'm scared to hear the answer. I don't know why I thought to ask this on her birthday.

"Yes, my loves, but Joel has to find an apartment. He's

probably going to move to the North Shore."

I'm shocked. On my mom's birthday, my dad stops being my dad. He's Joel now. He becomes a stranger in her mouth. Following this, my mom leaves our party to join the friends who are waiting for her in the yard.

A period of weightlessness. I become more interested in femininity. In Manon's and Michelle's many pairs of shoes. I especially like the highest heels, the stilts as I like to call them. When I try them on in secret, I am a tall woman who can see further than the horizon. I overcome the sadness of the boy who weighs me down. I also like the crimson red shoes that reveal the tops of my porcelain feet and my delicate ankles.

With Michelle, I dress up, I perform living-room theatre. Olivier remains in the background but he comes to the premieres with Charles and Manon. They have front-row seats to the definitive beginning of my passion for acting. Michelle lets me look through her accessories and I fall in love with her blue scarf. She takes out her camera and we lip-synch to Dalida, The Platters, and Petula Clark. *When you are alone, you can always go downtown.* Going to the city is heading to where life is happening.

Michelle's boyfriend comes to get her in his shiny car. I watch the planes that pass by. Each white trail is a thread to keep the sky from falling.

Michelle lets me choose her accessories when she goes out. Friday nights are always filled with an infectious excitement. She crimps her hair. Sprays it with hairspray. Nothing moves, even if she shakes her head to her favourite rock bands. Big rings dangle from her ears like flaming hoops.

After kissing me on the forehead so it leaves a mark, she leaves the house and goes to meet her boyfriend. I feel like I've been blessed.

She offers me a collection of lipsticks to try on. A brick red, a velvety peach, a pearly beige, a garish fuchsia, a candy pink. I imagine a slew of men at my feet, fascinated by the colour of my lips. In this way, I become visible. Unavoidable. I think about Michelle's bust. I'm jealous of her shape.

While searching through her drawers I find a vinyl skirt. I touch the material that feels like liquid, delighted when it gets warmer in my hands. I decide to try on the miniskirt over my pants.

"What are you doing with that on?"

Michelle's boyfriend has come in without my hearing him. When I eventually realize I should ask him to keep it to himself, he says, "It looks pretty good on you. It's a special combo, skirt-pants!"

He gets closer to me and I back up. He tickles my ribs, and the more he does it, the more alive I feel. I know that I will sleep well tonight. He leaves with Michelle's purse, which he had come to get. I get up on the little stool by the window and I pull aside the curtains to watch them together. She waits for him on the hood of the car while smoking a cigarette. Distracted, I wobble and fall to the ground. It makes a ruckus.

"Are you okay?" asks Manon.

Am I ever. I just fell over from the happiness of finally being recognized.

Manon brings Olivier and me to the outdoor public pool. After swimming, I head to the reception to get a soft drink. Wrapped in a giant towel, I can walk around, sheltered from people looking at my body. The only thing they can talk about is this travelling towel that comes from the far end of the village. They can only see my ankles and my feet, as well as my neck and head. I'm sure I look like a mascot. The pool manager, behind the counter, is sitting on a couch and watching a soap opera on TV. "The machine is broken, sweetie." Manon comes in while he's saying this. "She can't get a soft drink today," he tells her, pointing at me.

"Oh, he's a little boy, not a little girl," she says warmly.

I stare at the tiles so I don't have to see the man's embarrassed look.

Sitting by the pool, I can't find my shadow because the sun is at its peak. Manon is on the phone with my mom.

"Yes, I can keep them for as long as you want. Plus, they get along with Michelle. And they're so well behaved… Oh yeah? Already? But doesn't Bernard have his own house?"

It's all I hear and it's already too much. Everything sinks into the sand, including my mom's voice, reaching me through the echo of the phone. The other kids take their parent's hand to go somewhere. I make my way alone, in the shadow of my mom.

I walk barefoot on the shower tiles with groggy, uneven footing. The water runs down the drain and I wonder if I can follow it. When I get out of the shower, I come back to the world, purified for a moment from the anxiety of not knowing anything.

It's a time when I don't ask any questions because I know no one has any answers.

A few weeks later, Dad moves to the North Shore. We hear that he has a new girlfriend. The divorce procedures move forward. Bernard is now living in our house. I don't want to go back. I'm happy at Charles and Manon's, finally. However, I move back home not long after my stepfather moves in.

Olivier takes refuge in video games. The woods are no longer inhabited by our creative enthusiasm. I feel like I'm becoming older, no longer a little girl, and that scares me.

Literature is my refuge. Hundreds of stories flash before my eyes. Manon is kind enough to bring me books from time to time. I devour everything off her bookshelf. I then head to the local library with her and come out with five or six books under my arm. I read until my eyes sting and burn. Dear writers, please accompany me through the thickest of silences. I try to bury my own history under theirs. When I can't play outside, I start to play myself from within. Don't keep quiet. Don't leave me to the randomness of the heart that no longer knows how to pump love.

I continue to write. In my stories, my long-awaited father returns; he gives me a Barbie as a present, and my mom's bruises no longer exist.

One fine morning, Mom discovers Pénélope under my bed. She takes her by the arm and shows her to me like she's a pariah. "Since when do you have this doll?" she yells.

That morning, Pénélope is thrown in the garbage. My tears can no longer join hers. Hands resting on the living room window, I watch the garbage collectors throw my doll in their truck and quickly leave. I reassure myself that at least she got to escape the family hurricane.

Mathias has abandoned his paper airplanes for remote-controlled ones. He invites me to hang out sometimes on a hill overlooking the river. Melissa comes with us and it irritates me. The plane flies over my uncertain fate, never to land in my territory again. When they kiss, I leave and let all sorts of voices fill me.

On the phone, I can hear my dad's girlfriend in the background. "We're going to be late for the flight."

He speaks to my mom briefly. It always ends in a shouting match. My dad sends me birthday cards. Olivier doesn't bother reading his. They are brief, almost casual. My card has the Bellas Artes building in Mexico City on it, a building that looks like a temple. The angel statues look happier and more peaceful than the ones in our churches. The building stands out against the too-blue sky and under the message, it's signed Joel and Claudine. I now know the name of the woman who will have to bend over backwards to gain my love.

"To you, my dear son, whom I think about even if we're far apart. Sending you some sun from Mexico."

Two sentences on a card to remind me that he's not here with us.

It's our first winter without Dad. The first Christmas. Already, I think about him promising to call me. I wonder how it will go.

Snow fell in large batches over the past week. The fir branches are heavy and look sad under the weight. There's only a little bit of sun today. I squint every time it's sunny. The snow's bright glare assaults me.

I spend a long time throwing myself into the snow. Unlike all the kids my age, who use their arms and legs to make angels in the winter white, I am so still I'm silent, and so I make angels that don't move.

When I look at the sun for too long, little black spots form and obstruct my vision. This bright star doesn't bring back my dad; it enrages me. I would love for things to be simple for once. My dad will emerge out of the night with his gladiator sword and come meet me. I close my eyes and the spots flicker, sometimes orange, sometimes red. I follow them. They bring me to the secret hiding place of my cries.

My butt wet, I tell myself that I'm going to get a UTI. It's what my grandmother always says. Later on the phone, she reminds me again after having wished me a Merry Christmas. I will have to drink cranberry juice.

Olivier has been busy building a castle for the past two hours. I'm impressed by the speed with which he erects the walls. I don't feel like building anything. I actually feel like destroying everything. If I could kick the house and turn it into dust, I would do it. I almost don't care that my mom is still inside.

Through the window, I can see my mom talking on the phone. She still walks around when she's talking to someone. With the reflection of the trees behind me, it's like the snow is actually in the house and the forest is too. It's funny. I see myself in the living room, in my snowsuit; my mom passes right through me and doesn't even notice. She's like an untroubled Snow White before meeting the witch. I might be the witch. Maybe I'll be the one to drive her crazy for good. She doesn't know that I'm planning to put sharp pins in Bernard's boots or maybe destroy the horticultural equipment he keeps in the garage. I build a sort of mental protection so that she can't read my mind. She whirls around with the phone in her hands. It's obvious that she's talking to one of her friends since she's been talking for so long.

I've had the same winter gear for two years. My legs are growing, but to compensate, my mom gives me large wool socks so I don't catch a cold. "We don't have the money for new boots, not yet."

After having made two or three angels that will stay frozen during a boring winter, I decide to go in. Snow falls off me onto the floor. "Hey there, pay attention! Clean up your mess!" yells my mom, blocking the mouthpiece with her right hand.

When she turns her back to me, I kick the clumps of snow under the couch with my woolly socked foot. My feet start to defrost. Olivier comes in not long after. He gets undressed on the mat at the entrance, puts away all his things. He offers to hang up my snowsuit with his, in the basement near the woodstove.

When she uses knives to cook, I still get nervous. We never talked about what happened at the flea market again, but I think about her crazy and vacant look that day, full of wind, and it still troubles me. I'm afraid I've inherited her crazy gene. It might have been the fine line between genius and madness that she wanted to trace on her finger.

We're cooking salmon pie.

"Mom, we ate that for Christmas last year."

"Go play outside if you're not happy then."

It's true that, inside, I can't really play. Inside, I have to deal with the voices in my head that keep telling me to run away.

Mom puts on a record, Joe Dassin in concert with the Red Army choir. It's practically all the classics that she adores but with a plethora of voices. The voices clear a path through the branches of the tree, brush against the glittering garlands, and move the figures in the manger. They knit together, only for themselves, a semblance of Christmas. It's like being in church. Oh, how happy my mom is at this moment! She moves her hips and Bernard takes her by the waist; I feel like leaving them to their intimacy but it's also this mother that I've always dreamed of seeing. I'd just love if her happiness were contagious.

There will be plenty of people over later. It stresses me

out and so I play with the red piece of skin on my thumb with the nail of my index finger. I pull on the skin, a little bit of pain goes through me; it still hurts less than my parents' fights. Though they're no longer together, their fights persist in my memory. Now it's my right thumb's turn. I chew my nails. It makes me angry because I can't let them grow as long as Michelle's. Anxiety is an ever-hungry beaver.

I hate Bernard because he always reminds me of my dad's absence. He likes me a lot though. He told me earlier this morning that he got me a present. I might like it.

Company arrives. My mom's friends, men and women dressed up, but not overly so. One of them is wearing jeans with holes in them, and a dinner jacket; another has on a dress with sneakers. Bianca and her long acrylic nails. She looks like a panther. They drop the bottles of wine, the chips, the appetizers, and the dips on the counter. All at once, there's no longer any space.

Manon comes by with Michelle, who's holding on to her boyfriend's arm. The one who caught me trying on one of Michelle's skirts. I hope he didn't tell her anything. He let his hair grow and I wonder if I shouldn't do the same. It falls halfway down his neck and he parts it down the middle. Michelle has become a platinum bleach blonde like Madonna, who's copied Marilyn Monroe, who's surely copied someone else.

Mom speaks loudly and above everyone else. She chain-smokes cigarettes. She's been dipping into the alcoholic punch since the beginning of the night. "My youngest put the clementines into the punch, it was a good idea, I think it's the fruit that absorbs alcohol the best! Ha ha ha!"

Mom laughs so loudly that she makes me jump every time.

The guests chase her laughter into the next joke.

"Go get the devilled eggs. Offer them to our guests, my boy."

"Go put away the coats, will you?"

"Go put the boots in the bathtub."

I feel like I'm in the army. I'm running everywhere, between the adults' legs. They often block my way because they don't notice me. There are so many people that sometimes I slip under the couch to get to my destination. Despite myself, I wade through the puddles of melted ice. My elbows are wet.

Mom changes the record and puts on Nana Mouskouri's Christmas album, with its high notes that coo like a nightingale.

"Come on, Émilie. It's so corny," someone complains.

"Yeah, put on some Elvis for us," says another.

Mom doesn't listen to them and they end up forgetting that they don't like the music.

They continue laughing. We put a party together as best we can. I'm the only one who can't bring herself to laugh like that.

I wait for my dad's phone call. He promised he would call. I wonder how he dances with that other woman. Does he tickle her sides like he did with Mom before the storm? I wonder why we love each other if it just leads to hate afterwards. Even at this age, I tell myself: It's better to have nothing so you have nothing to lose.

Olivier's hair is slicked back with Dad's gel (he forgot it in the medicine cabinet in the bathroom). He smells like my dad, and I hate him for reminding me of him. Look at him trying to grow up too quickly. Because it's Olivier, I won't shove him on the staircase. Sometimes, when I'm sick of going up and down the stairs, I sit at an angle on the banister and slide down. It makes me feel like Mary Poppins, happy for the duration of the slide. When I put my feet on the ground, I regain my balance. One time, in the evening, I missed the last step and flew back against the wall, stifling a groan. I didn't check to see if I was injured; instead I checked if someone saw me because that's what would hurt most.

Mom takes out the champagne. Something that looks like it, in any case. She and her friends yell loudly, and we almost can't hear Nana Mouskouri anymore. Michelle's boyfriend almost crushes my foot with his large waxed black shoes. He didn't see me because I was on all fours. He turned around and apologized profusely. I was flattered by the attention.

I reach everyone's belly buttons. I would blow into them if I were in a better mood. I would go back outside if my snowsuit wasn't wet or if my angels would stop crying senselessly.

Mom is even more tipsy. Her cheeks are redder than her nice-smelling blush. She walks around with a tray. "Champagne, hard liquor, beer, *anéting, anétime*, it's party!"

It's like she's done this her whole life, which is sort of the case, except usually it's pills rather than alcohol she's serving on a tray.

A rumour circulates that Santa is coming this evening—for Olivier and me and all the adults who don't want to grow up, all the Peter Pans of this world who might burn if it were only up to me. I would take Michelle's lighter from the right pocket of her little leather coat, which was dropped off on the bed earlier. I would set fire to all the coats. I like that fire dances. All of the guests would have to leave in the December cold with nothing on their backs. Olivier looks at me. He knows I'm planning a dirty trick. It disarms me on the spot. I cancel my plans. If Mathias were here, it would be easier. He would pretend to have a heart attack or be allergic to salmon and the fire would slyly come alive in my mom's room. All this, I note in my head. Mathias wouldn't be able to believe I was so imaginative. He would idolize me. I would be his queen, the one for whom he would do the impossible.

Mom almost falls with the tray in her hands. I thought she was more solid on her little bird legs.

"You should go lay down a bit, my love. We haven't eaten yet," recommends Bernard. "Santa's showing up after supper. You didn't forget, I hope?"

I look at her red nose that makes me think of Rudolph the Red-Nosed Reindeer. In my overalls with the little red buttons that have four holes each, I laugh. Fake buttons, that way they'll never fall off. I won't lose them down the cracks in the couch, under the seat of the car, or in the vacuum.

The bathrooms are constantly occupied. I'd like to go pee outside, for once pee standing up, write my name in the snow, but I'm worried that I'll freeze from my penis up to my heart. I hold it in. Santa's coming anyway. I'll get some presents. I wasn't good. In any case, I know it, but no one in the room knows I was ready to set the house on fire. I imagine that my mental protection spell will conceal me from Santa's keen eyes, which scrutinize the actions of all the kids in the world.

There's a knock on the door. My orange juice (I'm obviously not allowed to have any punch) trembles in my hands. Santa enters the room. Everyone stops talking before screaming in chorus, "There he is!" I only see the gift he has for me in his overflowing pouch. Everyone applauds like he's Joe Dassin. But he hasn't come back from Europe, he hasn't succeeded in softening my heart, and he hasn't brought back my dad.

"Go stand beside the tree. It'll be your turn soon," orders my mom.

I'll fall into the tree with the glass balls if the others don't move over. I steal a devilled egg off the plate of someone I don't know so I can devour it within seconds—if only all my problems could disappear that way. The guy whose egg I stole is wondering where it went. I'm like the punk music Michelle records onto tapes with her boyfriend sometimes, except I don't have a stop button.

I need to go to the bathroom. The orange juice I swallowed too quickly is putting pressure on my bladder. The second I decide to go, I'm called to sit on Santa's lap. The cameras are out; they want to see what someone who still believes in something looks like. I feel like I'm in a documentary about sadness. I force myself to smile. He smells like cigarettes. Dad still hasn't called me.

They look for my present in the bag for an eternity. During this time, I notice that Santa smells kind of like Bernard's cigars. He even has the same eyes as him. I whisper in his ear, "I know it's you, Bernard."

His eyes widen. Surprised at being discovered. I smile at him. Deception is reserved for adults. I realize I've just joined the adult world, despite myself, and from now on, they won't be able to trick me. It makes me feel disdained. Seeing Bernard uncomfortable makes me smile. My mom notices. No one knows what I'm doing. Not even Bernard. I smile even wider, so much so that my mom hurries to get her Polaroid to immortalize the moment. The flash resounds in the house. Now, I'm smiling with teeth. Because of the costume's thickness, Bernard doesn't yet know that I'm emptying the entire contents of my bladder onto his lap.

The next summer, my mom and I visit my grandmother in Québec City. Trips to that city are rare; it's exciting to get away. It'll be a little vacation from my too-silent village and a break from Bernard as well. We've arrived in the city. I slept here and there along the highway, to soft and steady percussive sounds as my head leaned on the side of the car. The smog makes the city look like it's in a bell jar. It's hard to breathe; Mom lowers the window to cool us down. I notice all the graffiti on the buildings. I sink into my seat, intimidated by the vastness of the city.

I walk alongside my mom. She talks to me about Bernard, again. It's exhausting to hear her nonsense. At the end of the winter and in the spring, a social worker visited Olivier and I every two weeks to see how we were adapting to the divorce. At school, we were called "dangerous" because we had a hard time controlling our anger. People don't talk to us much because of the divorce. They don't know what to say, and so it's better if they don't say anything. Cars pass by at full tilt along my grandmother's street.

"Damn it, they could have hit us."

Mom pulls herself together. The hustle and bustle of the city fascinates me. Everywhere I look, something is happening. There in front of us, a man is walking his dog. To the right, kids are playing hopscotch. On the other side of the road, a dozen cyclists with numbers on their jerseys are waiting at the red light. It's a far cry from the boring calm of the countryside.

Two Japanese lilacs brighten her front yard, greeting us with their fragrant white panicles. Grandma planted these shrubs in the seventies, when she and Grandpa first moved in.

"You have such nice cheeks! Come here," she exclaims from the porch, as she watches me walk up. She's wearing her Sunday best: a beige miniskirt and her light, white, knitted short-sleeved top. Her golden mane has been freshly styled for the occasion. I take in all the beautiful things she tells me. I make them into provisions that I'll quietly bring back to my empty home.

We enter the apartment.

"Sorry for the mess, I decided to change everything around. But what with my hip hurting, I didn't think that it would take me twice as much time."

All of the day's heat stagnates in her small one-bedroom, even though the windows are open. The smell of asphalt lingers in the room. I wrinkle my nose.

"Oh yeah, it smells, eh? They are redoing the backyard with new asphalt. But hold on, I'm going to light my lavender candle."

Grandma has a solution for everything, it's so nice to see her at it. She's still full of life despite her pain.

We walk through the neighbourhood after supper, while Grandma has a nap. In an alleyway, there are two men built like tanks. To my great surprise, they are circling around a person slumped on the ground. They kick her and punch her. We can hear wheezing. They circle like vultures but they're voracious like hyenas. The violence doesn't stop. My mom and I are stunned. I notice that the person they're beating up is a man in a dress. The person on the ground begs them to stop, and my mom pulls on my arm to speed up my pace. I'm shocked that we don't intervene.

"In the city, you have to handle things on your own and, above all, you don't get involved in other people's business."

"But Mom, the man needs help."

"I don't know why your grandmother stays in this city."

We are back at the apartment. We watch TV but I'm not able to concentrate. Mom hasn't spoken about the scene we just witnessed. I'm unable to think about anything else. I hear the cry of despair. By not doing anything, we still pushed that someone off the cliff. Grandma ends up recounting memories from when she was pregnant with my mom. Mom rolls her eyes.

"In that case, I'm going to go smoke a cigarette…"

I still can't stop thinking about the person who was assaulted in the alleyway. It feels like she's with me.

"You're miles away right now, aren't you?" Grandma asks me in her velvety voice. "I have a little something for you, wait a couple seconds."

She comes back, taking her usual little ballerina steps, with a rose quartz pendant that she hangs around my neck.

"It's funny, this gem was at Charles and Manon's. I wanted one of my own."

"I've wanted to give you this for a long time now. Since your birthday is fast approaching but I can't be there for it, now's the right time."

My eyes widen. I feel a soft heat in my chest, as though my heart has suddenly learned how to breathe.

"Each time you're scared, don't forget this stone of love. Stay in loving state, stay confident. It will show you the way. It's a gemstone I brought back from Mexico ten years ago."

In the meantime, my mom comes back. "God, you and your esoteric stuff."

My grandmother doesn't pay her any attention. She approaches me, smiling as she whispers, "When your grandfather and I separated, I needed to recharge. I decided to go to Mexico and I met a shaman there who was selling pendants by the beach. I spent the night awake and listening to the waves and crying. The next day, I went back to see the shaman. I asked him to make me a pendant and to pick the stone that spoke to what my heart needed. He chose rose quartz to heal my heartbreak. I know it's not always easy at home, that separations are often traumatizing, but sometimes, it's necessary so that flowers can bloom. Charles told me you liked gemstones. I felt like I needed to give you this pendant to help you through all of it. There." She kisses the pendant. "This way, I'll always be with you."

I take in everything my grandmother tells me. I can see her on the beach trying to decipher what the sea has to tell her. I hold my gift tightly against my heart. I won't ever take it off. It's already so precious.

"Alright, that's very nice but we have to go. Make sure to put that necklace under your shirt, okay? Pink is for girls and the other kids will make fun of you at school."

I think again about the vultures in the alleyway. I hold my pendant tightly. I already feel better.

I'm starting high school, a world both strange and terrifying. I'm excited I finished elementary but here I am, thrown into a world where all the teens from all the villages in the region come together in one place. Still, my stomach aches and I'm stuck in the bathroom right up until we leave that morning.

Olivier is already used to this faster pace of life. "Hurry up, it's not like elementary. The bus driver won't wait around for us if we're late."

The most stressful thing is going from being the oldest at my elementary school to this vulnerable embryo in the eyes of the older kids.

The school doesn't look anything like what I've gotten used to over the past six years. It's at least four times bigger, and instead of looking rustic, it has more of a concrete look, almost like a prison. There's a large lot where dozens of buses are stationed in tight rows, ready to take us back home. There's a roundabout with greenery in front that they all pass through. Trees, mostly ash and birch, cast everything in their refreshing end-of-summer shade. The school is on a hillside, and behind it, a winding woodland is ready to be discovered by those curious enough. Unlike elementary school, there are no fences here, and yet I feel like I'm going to jail.

Inside the school, it's easy to get lost in the maze of immaculate white hallways. I'm going to be spending the next five years of my life here. I keep asking for directions. I'm promptly pointed in one. But where is "that way"? I end up in front of the library, and immediately it becomes my salvation and my refuge.

I'm afraid of going out into the world. I make sure to follow another student in my class when we have to get to our classes. I spend high school stuck behind someone's back. I'm not with my friends from the village; I'm in this hazy new reality. They spread us out into different classes to "encourage socializing between regions," says the principal in his grey three-piece suit, which matches the school concrete.

I see Mathias during breaks and at lunch. I can hardly eat because my stomach is in knots. He's going out with Melissa. They're always holding hands. I already mourned the possibility of a relationship with Mathias last summer, when I realized he only had eyes for her. He plays with her hair. They often laugh together, and sometimes I surprise myself by laughing with them. That's just the way it is.

They play rough near the lockers. The guys try to prove their physical superiority. Some fight in the corner. No one looks at them; they are part of the decor. From now on, a certain violence is part of our everyday life. I'm shoved while being called a bag of bones. In the bus, when I'm sleeping, I'm woken up by bits of erasers being thrown at me. I'm a little shaken up, like a bear coming out of hibernation. I don't look behind me. I know they want to erase me out of existence. I think about it, more and more.

I always feel depressed when I have to go to my locker. I practised unlocking my combination lock at home a week before school started to get fast at it and be able to get out of school as quickly as possible.

I run around in gym class like a lab rat. I wonder why we don't go running in the large fields near the school. In the locker rooms, I don't get changed in front of the others. I remember the lake at summer camp, and the thought is enough to terrorize me. I'm worried that others will look at my body, analyse it, shamefully dissect it. I'm afraid of being at the mercy of sniggering and all of a sudden not knowing how to get away, so I'm always on the alert, always ready for a threat to emerge. I'm worried they'll see my chest.

"I think he never showers…" one of the guys exclaims after realizing I never change after gym class.

And once again, my reputation as dirty is renewed for another innumerable amount of years. I don't perspire like the other guys, brimming with testosterone. No, my sweat leaks inside me.

To save myself from the torture of gym class, I decide one day to go see the school nurse. She looks grave and has a grey perm. She always seems busy with paperwork. I wonder if she's at ease here, if she likes it in this prison. I don't know if I'll be able to lie. She has X-ray vision. The idea of going back to class makes me so nauseous that, finally, I turn pale. I want to vomit out all my shame.

French is still my favourite class. I like the teacher. She always has little brooches in her silver hair. She reminds me of an owl who seems to know everything. She passes near us and lowers her gaze to look over our written work.

I raise my head. After having read some sentences, she nods at me approvingly. I'm her favourite.

There's a guy who looks at me often, and I know because I often look at him too. His name is Thomas. He has a colouring pencil behind his right ear and draws in the margins of his notebooks. He's always dishevelled and doesn't seem preoccupied with what others think of him; I admire him for this. He's most radiant when he's concentrating on one of his drawings. He often asks me for the assignments because he never listens to the teacher. I repeat all of the instructions in his ear with my little trembling voice, unseen by anyone else.

A few weeks later during our first group project, to my great surprise, he asks if I want to partner with him. I'm euphoric; for once, I'm approached for something other than being teased. Thomas leans on my desk to write his phone number on a piece of paper. The bell rings. I surrender to the din of the classroom. I stare at the smiley face that he drew beside his name.

I find out, during our meetings at lunch, that he comes from the town the school is in. He is the son of a government employee who works at the courthouse. I wonder why he's interested in a boy from the edge of the village who no one can figure out. I meet him on weekends at a fast food restaurant. We exchange shy looks over our fries. We work on our homework. When he laughs, I feel like sleeping peacefully on his freckle-dotted cheeks because they seem so soft. One day our hands touch, away from prying eyes. We go for walks in the woods during breaks at school. Then we race back to our classes. Our laughter smells of peony flowers and cedar boughs.

I don't feel like controlling the myriad sensations that inhabit me. When I get home, I hope no one speaks to me, so that I can replay those precious moments with him.

"I find it cute, the way your little ears stick out."

"I was also called a monkey in elementary, because I climbed everywhere."

It's nice to be electrified by his beauty. It gives meaning to my days.

In between the branches, I hear someone say that smoking stops growth so I ask an older girl for a cigarette. I think that if I get taller later on, I'll be less feminine. I'm not done growing yet. I want to stay smaller than Thomas so that he can wrap his arms around me, and I can hide my head in his chest and hear the beating of his heart. My throat burns; I might choke on this smoke but I tell myself I'm doing it for my own good. I think about Michelle, who gracefully exhales the smoke. I'll be like her, joined by Thomas on the hood of a car.

We pass a cigarette between friends during breaks. We're under an awning, sheltered from the sun and the rain. I feel like I'm part of a group. I like raising my face to the sky when I exhale the smoke. I think I look like those movie-star actresses. Thomas steals a couple puffs off me. We kiss through smoking the same cigarette. We chew gum and go back to our classes, proud of doing something forbidden without our parents' knowledge.

Thomas looked at me several times. I smiled at him and we passed that smile back and forth. I felt like we were playing a game of ping pong.

Thomas thinks I have nice eyes. He doesn't know it's because they're always more pretty when I'm looking at him. Otherwise, they are colourless and have no spark.

I was once again called anorexic at lunchtime.

I start weighing myself every day. I eat like a fanatic so they'll stop insulting me, but later the guilt returns and I dig my fingers into my throat to make the bile come up. I try to do this without anyone noticing. Sometimes, when I can't hide it because someone else is at home, I go throw up in the forest. I examine myself in mirrors and scrutinize the devastating effects of adolescence on my childhood body. My shoulders have widened at the same rate as my fear. I imagine sleeping every night rolled up in plastic wrap so I never become as big as an adult. I have to convince myself that I like my body, that I like the pubic hair that starts to appear, this Adam's apple that snatches away the voice I loved. My body is an insult.

Thomas and I have almost finished our project. I have this nagging fear that he'll lose interest in me when we finish it, so I take my time so as not to finish it too quickly. We send each other tons of messages in the middle of class. Papers folded and refolded hundreds of times. We shoot each other glances to synchronize the moment we'll both drop our pencils, to drive the history teacher crazy. It makes me think of those moments of pure friendship I shared with Mathias, except we're not breaking any windows. With him, I open windows that look out onto a peaceful existence.

On the way home from school, we take a path through the woods. Thomas seems to want to tell me something. He keeps opening his mouth as if to start talking but he ends up just coughing. The silence scares me because, in my family, it always signals bad news.

The moment I turn around to ask him what he wants to tell me, he gives me a peck on the cheek. "I've been wanting to do that for a long time…"

I don't speak, stupefied by this display of affection. I touch my cheek to try to keep his kiss there for longer. We're under an ash sparkling with the end of the day's light, and I just received my first kiss on the cheek.

"I hope I didn't make a mistake," he worries, and I return his kiss with one of my own.

We're under the spell of the kiss. We get to his house and I feel like I'm not touching the ground anymore. His mother is in the living room and gets up as soon as we arrive. She has such black eyes that you can't see her pupils. Her equally black hair has the bluish sheen of night. She makes us salmon on a bed of rice.

"Can we drink a little bit of wine with supper, Mom?" asks Thomas.

She seems hesitant but decides to pour us a cup each. I don't know why there are so many utensils by my plate, and I start to feel nervous. During supper, I wait until someone else picks one up before copying them. We eat on gold-rimmed plates. We get an appetizer, a velvety squash soup, then a Greek salad—I devour the feta pieces first. I discover my love for salty foods; later it'll be the salt on skin. It's the first time I have wine. It goes to my head pretty quickly. I want to kiss Thomas all over. The salmon melts in my mouth and I wonder how his mother cooks so magically. I've never had a dish this good. The dessert is a Queen Elizabeth cake that disappears as quickly as it arrives. After supper we go up to his room.

"You can sleep here if you like. I know you don't live very close by…"

I can tell that he's tense; I don't know what answer he wants from me. If I refuse, I'm afraid he'll think I'm not interested, and if I stay I'm afraid he'll think I'm easy. He swings back and forth like a pendulum, punctuating my indecision. I decide to call my mom to tell her that, actually, I'm going to sleep over. Thomas rejoices on his bed. Night follows the day.

Thomas approaches me and slips under the covers. I shrink back. I feel his breath on my face.

"Shh, it's nothing, it'll be okay."

I don't understand why he thinks it's nothing. It represents the end of my fantasy world. I see my dad in the blueberry field. Mathias tapping me on the shoulder to break my concentration as I fly his remote-control plane. Michelle on the hood of the car, exhaling her cigarette. Her boyfriend digging into my ribs, looking for my laughter. The schoolyard. The gym window shattering into a million pieces. My thigh scratched during the chase. The peroxide's foam on my wound. It all seems like it's from a different time now. Thomas bites the back of my neck. I see the person on the ground getting beaten up in Québec City. I don't know why I can't be present in this moment. It's like I need to be somewhere else. The potato cellar. The raccoon.

I look at my body and don't understand why I'm a boy. I want my dress right now. The black stains on the ticked boxes at the social worker's. A bird, a hammer, a whale, an angry father.

"I'm sorry for biting your lip."

I didn't feel anything. I concentrate on Thomas's fingers moving over my body. I can feel his touch. It's like he's making me real, a little more anchored in the world. His lips leave tingles wherever they go. It's so strange that this body I hate can give me pleasure. Its hollows, its mountains, its valleys. I exist under the pressure of Thomas's palms. Finally someone who is interested in me. Little blue bolts of lightning at the tips of our toes. His arms tremble. I offer my body in all the desire it arouses. A hint of bitterness finally appears. I realize that I don't know who I'm going to tell about my first time. My mom will certainly not approve of my secrecy. Mathias only has eyes for Melissa. My dad is still in I don't know which other country.

"Why are you staring at the ceiling?" Thomas asks.

I want to tell him that I can't be here, that I have to be somewhere else, otherwise it hurts too much. We end up falling asleep, spooning.

It feels like years go by, and we don't talk about what happened in his room again. At school, I give him some help since he has to repeat his tenth grade French class. For a week, we meet every lunchtime to revise his French for the exam that will decide his future.

We make a strange pair: Thomas, who often ends up in detention to finish his homework, and me, the angel, no one suspecting she wants to explode. I hold in my anger most of the time. Otherwise, I scribble on the walls of the bathroom and on desks. I never say it's me.

Every lunchtime is an opportunity to not be alone.

"You're the perfect guy for me. Thank you so much for helping me with this."

I don't feel good when I'm spoken to in the masculine. He scratches his nose, as allergic to spring as summer. We also see each other at his house. I play the part of the good friend so his mother doesn't suspect anything. The second we enter his room, we start kissing with fierce passion. He tells me about his plans. He wants to study architecture in Montreal. I find it impressive that he has a plan that projects him so far into the future. My own fogginess stops me from seeing as clearly. Maybe one day, he could give me advice on how to structure my chaotic existence. While sitting and having a beer, he asks me what I want to become. I tell him I want to become someone, a person under the spotlight who does good for those around her.

"To our excellent projects," he exclaims while clinking our beers.

Near the end of the year, he invites me to a party. He is expecting about twenty people, most of whom I only know by sight. Although I'm nervous about seeing people I don't trust, I accept the invitation.

I take long, meditative walks with Thomas, and it seems that in his company the noise in my head isn't disturbing.

Thomas has the house to himself for the evening. He is radiant, lit with a joie de vivre that I have never seen in him before. It moves me. I falter in the presence of his splendour.

I borrowed Michelle's eyeliner to line my lids with black and make my eyes look feline. It's the first time I've done it in public. I feel bold and fearful at the same time. My fear dissipates when Thomas comes to join me. "Wow, the eyeliner looks good on you. It somehow doesn't make you look emo!"

I offer him a smile, the biggest of my life.

The beer flows freely and the music follows. System of a Down plays at times, more often pop. We sweat to Cascada. I free my hips from their masculine rigidity. Wild, I sparkle on the dance floor. This attracts Thomas's attention, who is now dancing with me, all smiles and sweat. I want him, want our bodies together.

The hours accumulate like the people at the party. Thomas and I go up to his room to steal a few kisses away from prying eyes.

"I want to make love when everyone else is gone," he says, taking my face in his hands.

I feel at home like this. I don't know if he can see that my smoky eyes are filled with tears of joy.

We're running out of beer, so Thomas decides to take his car to go get more. He asks me to join him. I'm amazed by his little nose, wrinkling with every joke I make. He puts his hand on my thigh. I caress his forearm. His driving leaves something to be desired but it doesn't matter because there is no one on the road at this time of night. He skips a few stops to go more quickly.

I whisper in his ear, "Watch the road, Thomas."

"Hey, I thought of this earlier when I was looking at your eyes with make-up on and I thought that you'd make a really beautiful girl."

He studies me for a second.

"Yeah, a real beautiful girl."

I bask in the weightlessness of his desire, serene, like exiting hell.

I find out that we almost hit a moose that was crossing the 138. A woman with a cellphone in her hands tells me.

It all comes back to me. My head hits the glove compartment. I see a flash. There's a sharp tear of flesh and metal. I can no longer hear my voice. A thin stream of air barely manages to escape my lungs. Liquid runs down my forehead. I don't know if it's gas or blood. I want to scream but nothing comes out of my throat. I don't know if I'm dead. Thomas's eyes are closed, his head resting on the steering wheel. It doesn't look good. I manage to free myself from the seat belt that's holding me back.

The lady saw the car fall into the ravine. She's surprised that I don't have more injuries than I do. She just called an ambulance. Thomas moves a little. He coughs up blood. I tell him that help is on the way.

From now on, whenever someone shows any interest in my femininity, I will withdraw for fear of another accident. Despite the severity of the crash, we manage to get out without too many injuries.

At the hospital, after I'm examined, I'm given a bed for the night. My mom has been called and she arrives with Olivier, his face striped with tears. Thomas needs more medical attention; he has a fractured rib that nearly punctured his lung, as well as a broken leg. I ask to see him.

He's hooked up to a bunch of wires. My mom orders me not to linger too long. She gives him a dirty look because he put my life at risk.

Going back to school, for me, is as though nothing happened. I lug Thomas's books for him; he's on crutches for the rest of the year.

At the beginning of the summer holidays, while having a beer, he tells me that he's moving to Montreal to study architecture. This news hurts me more than the accident. I didn't know then that it would be the last time I would see him.

Sometimes I wake up at night to the screech of tires and Thomas's cry upon impact. It's been two months since the accident. I decide to sign up for Facebook because no one is talking about anything else. The site suggests some friends. I skim the profiles without interest. I like the fact that I can share my writing. I share poems, most of the time written between two anxiety attacks. I notice there's a guy who always reacts to my posts. This is how I meet Guillaume. I decide to go check out his profile and discover a myriad of music videos he's posted in which he improvises guitar riffs using his electric guitar. It's as though his heart is speaking through his fingers, the chords, and the music. It's a language I understand.

Over time, the videos thread themselves into my routine like a soundtrack. I get home from school, shed my belongings at the bottom of the stairs, and hurry to watch his newest upload. Sometimes at night, I check to see if he's posted anything so I can have new music to fall asleep to.

I browse his photos. Always this sad look. I look for a smile but it seems to have never been there or maybe it's been erased. At four o'clock one September morning, I decide to write to him. He responds to me right away. I confide in him, telling him about my separated parents, about my boredom in the countryside, about the sexual orientation I try as best I can to hide. We join each other in the chasm of the same sadness.

He senses that my angst burdens me. On his end, he says his parents don't know yet but that he'll get there; one day he'll find the courage. We return to the solitude that weighs on us, to the anxiety that torments us, to the uncertainty of our days. Our two solitudes unite to let light in. He sets my turbulent nights back on course. He knows how to finish my sentences when I feel like I don't know how to talk about myself anymore, about what I'm living, and especially about what I don't experience.

He lives in a hamlet on the edge of Québec City, on the other side of the bridge. He struggles to reveal his desire for other boys, even to his friends. On top of not liking the way I look and being afraid of disappearing if I don't eat enough, I also hate my heart for not knowing how to speak. I'm angry that I don't know how to express this thing that might kill itself if I can't figure out how to express it. To ourselves we are monsters, abominations; we understand each other in our marginalization.

We turn on our webcams. His emerald green eyes shine in the ocean of mine. He has long curled eyelashes that make him look like a doll, in contrast with the shape of his square face. Behind this structure of ruins hides a child that cannot stop crying. We send each other songs. Music is our shared language; we don't get to know each other through speaking. There's the music I show him that reminds me of certain smells. Joe Dassin's "Dans les yeux d'Émilie" reminds me of my mom's floral and exotic perfume mixed with kelp from our euphoric beach trips.

Mom used to take me by the hand and spin me in circles. Emotions well up when I talk about this period that seems to belong to another era. I need to take a break and write to Guillaume later. I make escape plans. It seems to me that I'm ripe for real life, real things. I want to fall from a tree, unlike my mom, in order to not rot in this village. This need to leave, to go far away, I inherit from my dad.

The more things change, the more they stay the same. Mom fights with Dad on the phone. Bernard suggests she cut him off. So then Mom fights with Bernard. She's always in conflict; if not because of a man, it's because of herself. When I see my mom on edge like this, I stab my nails into my thighs. It leaves crescent moons in my flesh. These nights remains on my legs for a long time.

Bernard smokes like a chimney. Everything reeks of it, even the curtains and the pillows in my room. My sleep is ablaze.

I take an interest in knitting to build a bridge between myself and the rest of the world. I'm productive, I pay back my anguish by selling scarves. I write to Guillaume from my room. The open window allows birdsong to inundate the space. This way, I don't hear the lovebirds in the living room.

They're over, the forest games, when it used to be easier to take refuge in characters. My responsibilities accumulate. Adolescence brings a heaviness that smacks me, quashing my childhood freedom.

My conversations with Guillaume become more and more effusive. He'd like to make a career of music, singing his own songs. For the time being, he has one foot in the music industry working as a sound engineer. He often goes to Québec City for the record label he works for. I propose we meet there for the first time. Finally I have a goal, going on my own. So I print a map of Québec, and I save my money for a bus ticket. I do my best to keep calm and hide my plan from my mom. I watch them during breakfast, her and Bernard; they seem happy, but my life is elsewhere. I think: in a couple of months, I'll be far away from you, and who knows, I might finally be closer to my true self. A few months later, I have the round-trip ticket in my hand and a big, full backpack.

"Today's the day I go visit Grandma," I tell my mom.

"Perfect, my love, be careful. Call me when you get there."

I squeeze my rose quartz pendant tightly, still always around my neck. As soon as I'm away from home, I'll take it out for all to see. I really do have to go to my grandmother's before meeting Guillaume to keep up the lie. My huge backpack makes me look like a turtle. My frail legs threaten to break from one second to the next. I packed my bag as though I'm leaving forever.

When I leave my mom at the bus station, I ask her if it bothers her that I'm going without her.

"You're old enough. I don't speak with your grandmother that often anyways, because she won't stop asking me for news about your father."

I feel a twinge in my throat.

It's my first time going to Québec City alone. The person in the seat next to me on the bus is a young businessman who is typing on a laptop. The continuous clicking of the keys stops me from thinking too much. I reread my conversations with Guillaume, which I printed before leaving. I think of dreams evaporating, dawn on my face.

Québec City reveals itself in the magnificence of summer. I look at my map once I arrive at the Gare du Palais. I'm in the middle of a procession of luggage and destinies. The hum of conversation is stupefying. The terror of getting lost is erupting in me. I stop often and sit on public benches, taking in big breaths. I'm dizzy. "You are not lost, you are finding yourself."

It's difficult to believe that I could be interesting enough for someone to want to see. I gave Guillaume the address of the mall near my grandmother's. We plan to meet tomorrow. The man on my screen is finally going to materialize in front of my eyes.

I'm in a taxi that's taking me to my grandmother. The counter rises at an alarming speed, and I worry about money. Stomach in knots, I throw furtive looks from left to right, as though Guillaume could be on a street corner a block away from my heartbeat.

If I can't pay for the taxi, I plan to make a break for it.

The taxi driver asks if I'm running away from home. I want to tell him I don't know.

I arrive at my grandmother's in time for her grocery run. Every moment I'm granted with her is precious. She has this reassuring presence that makes me forget my family troubles for a time. I give the lilacs a reverential curtsy as they greet me, arms filled with love. The apartment door on Lilas Road opens. My grandmother hurries forward with her contagious joy. She kisses me on the forehead several times, like a woodpecker.

"You're still wearing your pendant. It warms my heart to see it!"

We enter the apartment. She offers me cookies and gelatinous candies coated in sugar. Her walk is graceful. She walks with dainty mouse steps. We sip jasmine tea on the balcony. It's the golden hour and the day is stained with melancholy while we watch children play under the sun in the backyard. I used to be as small as them, a little girl, but I grew up at lightning speed.

"Hey, you have time to grow old, believe me, so make the most of your youth while it lasts."

She tells me stories about each child she knows. The load of whites on the clothing line hangs in the feeble afternoon breeze and makes me think of the still blank pages of my unlived stories.

I find out that in the city, both in the evening and at night, it's never actually fully dark because of light pollution. Shadows on the walls of my bedroom make me jump. I realize it's likely just the cars passing by. I see wild animals approaching me, so I don't sleep a wink. The tree's shadow, near the window, looms like tentacles waiting to pull me away from my happiness. Eventually, I even stop hearing my grandmother's snoring and I worry myself sick. It's the first time I've slept beside her, and I'm afraid she'll die in her sleep. I rush to the bathroom several times. I wonder how many ticks of the clock separate me from slumber.

The next day, the apartment recovers its pastel colour. Grandma parts the curtains and light shines right through the living room. We chat in our pyjamas. I can't sit still; I'm going to see Guillaume soon. I'm on the couch touching the leaves of her plants while she talks to me. The cool, waxy touch is pleasing, relaxing. Grandma melts butter in a pan. She's making French toast. The intoxicating aroma of milk and vanilla makes my mouth water. She sneaks glances my way, unaware that I see her every time. I let her do it because I know that it allows her to indulge in a tenderness that she doesn't allow herself to have with others. Nervous, I find myself rolling the bottom of the lace tablecloth.

"I know it will be fine," she says.

I push my chair back. She has this gift of reading my thoughts before I've even composed a sentence in my mind; that's why I love her. She wraps me in her arms and says something my mom rarely says to me, "I love you."

Once I've arrived at the mall, I find Guillaume right away, sitting on a bench. I gently tap him on the shoulder. He turns around and opens his mouth. For a second I feel like running away, but then relax under his gaze.

We decide to go to his place. Once we get there, we head to the kitchen in the basement. He's lived alone for a year. Guillaume adjusts his glasses, even though they aren't falling off his nose. I can tell he's nervous. I start to feel scared, I am far from home… and what if he has bad intentions? The fact that the kitchen is plunged in darkness adds to my concern. He turns on the light. I notice the static of a record. "Love Me Two Times" by The Doors is playing. He starts cooking supper. Pasta with Béchamel sauce. I have tears in my eyes when I see the floor. Rose petals adorn the ceramic tiles. Wisps of floral incense smoke waft between our smiles. When he sees how moved I am by all this, two suns rise in his eyes and banish any shadows that still live in me.

His movements are slow, precise, and fascinating. He's so different from me; I'm always on the move and never able to stay put. I admire the fact that he has his own apartment, his own freedom. He grates cheese. I clear my throat to fill the silences, though they aren't uncomfortable. I know I can trust him with my sleepiness.

Halfway through my plate of pasta, I can't help myself; I rush towards him. I emerge from the deep depths and finally find my breath. "L.A. Woman" plays; it will become our song. We roll in the petals, in this love that is coming alive and that will grow, I already know. It's a question of giving it our all, without hurting ourselves on the ceramic tiles.

He discovers my body. I'm ashamed of my sex, but not enough to not surrender myself to him. I want to spend my life with him.

We go out and stand on the porch for a while, the whole neighbourhood seemingly fast asleep. No dogs are barking. I'm entangled with him. Thousands of stars in the sky, the end of adolescence, are brightened by a new constellation: us.

The next day, after an idyllic evening, Guillaume is already driving me back to the station. I must not sow the seed of doubt within my family. The road is a smooth straight line, unlike the road in the countryside, bumpy and uneven. It's bittersweet to have met him. I dread a curse: the rest of the way I'm on the lookout, scanning our surroundings, hoping we won't come across any moose that might cause an accident. I clench my fists when we take the bends. I wonder what will hit me.

The trees unfold in a heat wave that sticks to my skin for a long time.

His face, between my hands, between my thighs. Here is the landscape of my new life.

It's the most graceful start to school imaginable. I float in the hallways. I no longer hear the taunting of my classmates. I only think about the next poems I will write for him. We email each other, dreaming of our lives taking on a new light. We draw up plans between the lines.

A few weeks later, when I get home from school, my mom is waiting for me. I notice that she has printed my emails with Guillaume. I realize foolishly that I didn't turn off my computer that morning. All of our conversations since we first met are in her trembling hands. She finds out that I can't wait to escape this "shithole," can't wait to see "what is hidden at the edge of the horizon," can't wait to free myself from the ambient doldrums that she has fuelled since my dad left, can't wait "to stop watching the theatre of her false love." That evening, my mom reprimands me. "How dare you speak about me like this when I've always given you everything you wanted? You could have ended up with a maniac. You never know, in this day and age. I don't understand how you're able to be so cruel to your own mother."

I don't know what to say, so I just sigh. I feel betrayed by my mom having searched through my computer. Each time we pass each other in the hallway, we argue.

"You can see a doctor to see if it's true. If you like guys. Maybe it's just a phase?"

My grades start plummeting. People repeat the guy name that no longer belongs to me. I want to wake him up, this boy who I'm not. Tap him on the shoulder and tell him to go live his life. But I also have the impression that he doesn't want anything to do with me, nor anyone else for that matter. I'm a girl watching myself from the sidelines, and I'm powerless.

I write poems in the margins of my notebooks. I skip classes. I walk near the train tracks and wonder if I have enough courage to jump onto the back of a train like in the movies. I dream about turning eighteen, so that my mom no longer has any influence over me.

I decide to try my luck at a film course that starts in Québec City in the next few weeks. To be able to enrol, I first have to pass an audition. Guillaume feeds me lines from the other side of the camera. It's the perfect opportunity to get out of here. I spend all of my free time memorizing lines.

When I get to the audition, I tell myself it's now or never. I have to land a spot in this class; if not, I'll rot in the village.

A bearded man, imposing in his massive stature, stands in front of me. A famous, internationally renowned actor who has become a teacher. Despite the pressure, I deliver my lines with a natural burst. The man approaches. I have to raise my head to look at him.

"Where have you been this whole time?"

I don't immediately get what he's saying.

"You've been accepted to the school."

All those hours spent in front of my mirror pay off, and I savour their sweetness. Before I leave the room to go back home, the man talks to me about my disarming naturalness. I tell myself that if the audition was a success, it's because, despite myself, I've been learning how to lie my whole life.

The countryside where I was born is gone, and so are the hills, the trees that sing, Mathias and our mean tricks. Thomas and the secret bedroom. Guillaume and I find an apartment in Québec City. My house, narrowed in my field of vision, becomes a pebble that will soon join my memories at the bottom of the pond. Mom waves in the rear-view mirror. I shed a tear. And another. And then I break down. Guillaume pulls my face up with his fingertips and looks at me for a long time. I think I'm going to see my mom cry even though she's already almost a kilometre away. You can just feel these things. My heart constricts. I don't understand my sadness; I was the one who wanted so badly to leave this village of a thousand scars. Nor do I understand this intense burst of anxiety which is here even though Guillaume is by my side and is telling me that he loves me. Even though I have everything I want.

Taking great care to prune the roots of our happiness as a couple, we fall into the patterns of our shared nest like a season. In the morning, we go for a jog in the park just behind our house. The trees swaying in the wind welcome us with open arms during this bright summer. In the afternoon, we unpack boxes. At some point, I open the one containing the porcelain figurines from my childhood. They have kept their smiles despite the darkness. I remember my mom hiding a ballet dancer figurine behind her back to surprise me. My mom's faded, cuneiform writing in old Sharpie remains on the box.

I also remember her washed-out, wedge-shaped, permanent love.

A month later, we take a road trip to Montreal. Some friends of Guillaume's invite us to a party. In that city, he can be himself; that city welcomes into its bosom all the people the world rejects.

Down there, it's possible to hold hands without worrying what other people will think, and it's an uncommon relief. I feel a bubbling in my chest. I'm effervescent in his company. We sometimes stop on the side of the highway. We take pictures. Our happiness exists everywhere; it's exponential. In the car, we listen to Queen, Smashing Pumpkins, Green Day. We stuff ourselves with candies we buy at little corner shops along the way. The views enter my lungs. Once there, I take all that the city has to offer: its parks, its fields, its alleyways at the end of the day, gilded with a summery caress. I roll my window down, stick my head out, and scream in happiness. The world unfurls in front of my eyes with the promise of a more peaceful life. I am free. Everything could fall apart around me but I'm at the centre with Guillaume, who grabs my ass while laughing.

It's a long way to Montreal, to live our love openly, but the kilometres are endurable, are relished. The huge city where buildings grow like flowers. I dream of going up to the roof of a building to touch the sky. Maybe up there my hopes for a happy life would become a priority.

Then we head to the bar. I follow Guillaume closely so that I don't lose him in the tide of people. It's festival season. The only thing that's missing is a festival of festivals. The roads are jam-packed. It's my first time taking the metro. A great, giant serpent devours the passengers. I hold on tightly to the stainless steel pole. My life is going as fast as the metro car. I think about Grandma, who told me to take advantage of my youth. I look at my pendant and I see her smile.

I watch people and people watch me. It's likely that they find me intriguing because of my worried expression. I must stick out from the rest of the crowd so used to this frantic rhythm. A labyrinth of streets and alleyways opens itself up to us and a city slalom begins. Situated in the Gay Village, the bar welcomes us with red and violet neon lights in the fresh breeze of the night. On the screens, there are videos of men in underwear or dressed from head to toe in leather. Guillaume orders two drinks at the bar. People pile in as the evening continues and we have no choice but to rub against other people if we want to get around. There's a room exclusively for men.

"Come on," Guillaume says.

I hesitate, I don't feel comfortable. It creates a tension that disappears quickly once "Living on My Own" by Queen starts playing on the dance floor. We dance to the lyrics about the freedom to be oneself. We hold each other tight. He grabs my hips, rolls them in his palms. Sweat seeps under his tank top. Everyone's smells mingle. I tease him with my feline eyes. I light a fire, this fire heats up my snow-covered prison. In the bathroom, Guillaume pushes me against a wall and kisses me passionately, and I discover a passion in him that feels like it's been buried for years. My body doesn't know how to take in so much love at once. I end up flowing with the current.

We take breaks. I let my head drop on his shoulder. I think of everything I was missing before I came here, this healing bloom I never allowed myself. I understand why Michelle felt so excited about this kind of outing.

It's fascinating to see men kissing without reserve; their freedom legitimizes my own. I release myself from the chains that I have polished for so long. A man kisses his own reflection in a mirror, the epitome of his self-love. I find out that there's a patio on the roof. At the top of the stairs illuminated by green and volcano-red neon lights, Montreal offers itself, sparkling and effervescent, and its children celebrate their existence. More than anything, its children aren't ashamed of who they are. It's new and, somehow, it's natural. A breeze softens our ardour. Here I am, at the end of the night, on top of this building, tickling the sky with the dreams I feed.

I'm in a party mood until I walk by a mirror. I stand there for a long time looking at this face assailed with hair. Who the hell are you? Why aren't you happy? Why do you keep struggling? My freedom disappears every time I look deep into my eyes.

It's time to go home. The road falls away under my heavy eyelids. In Québec City, in the early hours of the morning, people go about their business and I feel like I'm too much in this chaos of responsibilities. All I want is to sink into bed. We sink into each other, fully clothed under the covers, with a new, precious memory. Guillaume and I are living our love behind curtains, for the moment. But it's only a matter of time before our love breaks through the doors and windows. After having gorged ourselves on so much beauty, we realize that we also have the right to exist together.

A few months go by. Things evolve. Our dynamic changes. Routine develops subtly in our life as a couple. Guillaume often gets home from the studio exhausted, and therefore less receptive to my displays of affection. I take it personally.

"Don't worry about it, it's just a phase."

I'm guilty of thinking he no longer loves me. I spend my time looking at a gigantic ash tree outside my window. Perhaps it has seen Guillaume's thoughts and could give me an idea of what's going on. I hear their singing, the birds, and it's the only thing that brings me peace.

The film classes begin. We're a group of five, chosen for the autumn session. The room is small, so we have to be close, which makes me feel ill at ease. I find it exhausting to always be on camera for the improv exercises. It bothers me to see myself. My mouth is not my own, it doesn't move with my voice which emerges from the depths of adolescence. Vertigo. Nausea.

Who is this boy?

During one of the exercises, I need to play a man who beats his wife and then becomes suicidal. I have my first panic attack in public. A chasm forms. The air becomes thin. I'm scrutinized. Under the spotlight. On a table, they dissect my feelings. I don't know how to tell the others that this boy they see is about to die. The person on the screen is going to die and take with her the person I am and the person I am not. If only I had been wise. Maybe I should have held on to the raccoon in the cellar and demanded the reason for its visit. With its claws, it could be concealing the truth deep in its fur. The hairdresser's nails pass near my bangs. The scissor's jaw closes in on my childhood. I have a hard time breathing.

Michelle spins around in a ballerina pose. I feel like shoving her away; I hate her for being so beautiful and radiant. I cry, thinking about things like this. It's not me.

Guillaume and I sleep back to back. Something's wrong. Thunderstorms are brewing in the hollow of the silence. I'm short of breath. Who took it from me? An unease snakes its way down my throat and dries out my mouth. I trickle into the bottom of an unnamed ocean that we haven't yet discovered in this time of revolutions to come.

I head to the secretary's office, hugging the walls, in order to cancel my class immediately. I think only of fleeing, of disappearing. I will not stand by and witness my own agony for another second. Everything I try slips through my fingers. I tried to love my dad's absence and failed miserably. I wish I had been simple-minded and didn't care about what people would say or do. I would have liked for my parents to have loved each other with the same fervour with which I loved my doll. This weight on my shoulders, increased now with the guilt of having moved for nothing. I put my hands on my heart so that it doesn't slip away.

Our life as a couple suffers due to my lack of confidence. Increasingly tired and more of a burden, I sink into evasion. I have to find the sun behind my closed eyelids.

Nothing is conclusive. I scour all the job search sites. I spend long hours making calls, burning my eyes looking at my computer screen, doing breathing exercises. I pray, addressing who? I don't know. I no longer believe in the man who did not watch over the chaos taking place on his land. I pray to the stars, I pray to the cacti that I buy every day in the shop next door and put on my windowsill. I pray so that I'm able to love all the thorny things in my life that have pierced my desire to still be here, causing it to bleed. I pray for their resilient flesh, which has the strength to stand despite the drought, despite the headwinds and the boreal nights.

I scour the Internet for an air bubble in the sinkhole of my despair. I finally come across an ad looking for someone to work in the cosmetics industry. I say to myself: why not? There's no way I'm going back to school to suffer another round of anxiety attacks.

Guillaume works on an album reminiscent of The Doors. I get a call a week later. That evening, he plays me a private guitar concert and then we make love.

My first day working in cosmetics, I arrive restless. I stammer when I'm asked questions. I sell prestigious brands: Guerlain, Lancôme, Estée Lauder. My boss has neon nails that she taps on the counter.

"You're a really a good salesman."

I am in my element: enhancing what exists. I like being dressed all in black so that no one can see my shape. So that people ask themselves: is that a boy or a girl? I ask myself that same question, more and more. I float in this void of in-between and I enjoy taking shape before their eyes, each according to their personal discomforts.

The training for the job takes place in hotels. I'm the only guy among a host of female makeup artists. I never sleep before a training session because I'm anxious about feeling like an intruder. In the early mornings, I lie in bed comatose. My room smells like lavender to help me sleep, but nothing helps. I always suffer through this groggy state, a lack of sleep. The trainer has a beehive haircut. I can smell her hairspray from across the room. She's enthusiastic; she gesticulates like a gym coach. I see myself in the window and I think I look older because of fatigue. We preach cosmetic innovations; they are our new church and our daily bread, these products that we receive in abundance in bags filled with tissue paper. Products we might try once or twice before they end up in the garbage. All the women look immaculate. There is not a single hair sticking out of their ponytails or their buns. They notice I'm different very quickly.

"I find it cool that a guy is doing a female job. Things are changing," says a woman at the far end, a pencil sticking out of her bun.

Another woman thinks I shouldn't be here because I'm a man. She always looks at me like she wants to kill me. Everyone looks at me and I want to disappear immediately. There's a giant aviary in this hotel, an artificial forest, and I try to cling to the branches of its captive trees, telling myself that in an hour's time, I'll be able to take a breath of fresh air.

When I work, people call me Miss. I buy more and more makeup that I keep in a small wooden box. I love lining my eyelids with obsidian black and making my lashes into little rays of sunshine around my blue eyes. I apply gloss to my lips because lipstick isn't as discreet. It gives me a dewy mouth that smiles more than usual. On my eyelids, I try pale beiges to brighten my eyes, a subtle brown to bring out the blue of my irises, and when Guillaume isn't there, I try on turquoise, canary yellow, and amethyst eye shadows. I'm a cave set with precious stones; I shine when you look at me.

One day, Guillaume notices the box on my dresser.

"It's just samples for me to try on so I can advise my customers better."

"I'd like it if, in my presence, you didn't wear any makeup please."

I placate Guillaume but delve in my wounds. I shrink myself, fade, blur, I become transparent, clouded over.

I start using several different products on a daily basis without him knowing. I use foundation to hide the irritation I get from shaving my face every morning. I make my cheekbones look more prominent by playing with shadows and light. Makeup is my way of feeling in control.

Guillaume spends a lot of time with his co-workers after work. I get home in my uniform. He gets home, hugs me, and we prepare supper. In men's clothing, I feel like I'm wearing a costume. While chopping vegetables, I search for the strength and drive I used to have. I bloom at work, but my radiance fades when I come home and I don't know why.

"I don't really like it when you wear makeup."

I'm a little surprised because I realize he's noticed it since the beginning. He often gets impatient for no reason. He often leaves without telling me where he's going. He only comes back to sleep and leaves again early the next morning to go to work. A wave that doesn't make any noise. I make up for his absence with the memory of his laugh.

A co-worker invites me to a Halloween party at a bar. While shopping, my eyes suddenly widen. A display of wigs catches my attention. I imagine myself in all of them. I try to imagine what it would feel like to have long hair, that touch on my back I've been waiting for. I ask the salesperson if I can try one on. In front of the mirror, I'm enthralled by my face, framed by long braids. My eyes fill with tears. I meet the girl I'd like to become. I hurry to buy it.

"Oh, it's for a girlfriend."

I leave with the wig in my bag like a thief.

Guillaume is working late, so I dress up the way I want to. I don't transform myself; I find myself. I take out my makeup case and, with each passing of the brushstrokes, devote myself to my resurrection.

My co-worker and I are in evening wear. I'm not wearing a skirt because I think about Guillaume, who already doesn't tolerate makeup. I try my best not to upset him with my clothing. I opt for a pair of black skinny pants that highlight my rounded ass. I wear a discreet bra; a black spaghetti strap tank top that shows off my frail porcelain shoulders; and high heels that I found at the thrift store around the corner, a bit used, faded, but not so scuffed that it's visible in the darkness of the bar. The bar is situated in the heart of downtown; there's a show every night. It's the middle of the week but there's a crowd. It's a popular venue. In the middle of the party sweat, we sway our hips to pop hits from the '80s and '90s. I unwind to a remix of Madonna's "Like a Prayer." We sing at the top of our lungs. I sing my body to the end of my fingernails, manicured for the occasion. The alcohol enters me like fuel into an engine; I don't try to stop myself. I want the party to last forever, for us to dance further than the sun. The vibration goes through me, and I bubble with joy. I bump hips with my co-worker and the motion pushes her around, and it makes us laugh.

A man sidles up, running a hand along my waist. He leaves with a smirk on his face. His foxlike smile is inviting but I'm thinking of my lover and I don't want to screw things up.

"You're really pretty," exclaims my co-worker.

I ask her not to say anything at work because it would embarrass me if the others knew what was going on. She buys me a shot to celebrate my courage in dressing this way. I feel like it's my birthday.

We sit at a booth, and not long after, people that I don't recognize join us. They are as drunk as the night.

"Are you a model?" mumbles a man with a red beard between sips. The beer foam gets lost in his beard. I'd love to bury my fingers in it, to leave with him. "What's your name?"

I haven't thought about a woman's name before. To avoid embarrassment, I pretend not to have heard him by making a joke. I get up. I check out the other women in the room. I try to get their names. None of them resonate with me. I dive into the crowd. The floor sways. I'm on a river that doesn't yet have a name. I feel nauseous. I try my best to concentrate on the conversation. I could call myself hips, ass, mouth, boobs for the evening, not knowing how to be anything else for them. I'm not yet whole. I'm living in the moment.

A man, blurred around the edges, approaches me. "If I buy you a shot of Jack, will you give me a blow job?"

I burst out laughing, shocked. When I realize he's being serious, I hurry to rejoin my co-worker. I try to get her attention but she's lost in the mouth of a stranger. To her, I no longer exist. I have a hard time moving. I keep having to lean against things: a chair, a counter, someone. I'm like a duck out of water. I accidentally bump into several people. Even the coat check smells like puke. Someone hands me my coat and purse that I catch mid-air. I walk through a cloud of smoke, hurry, and vomit outside on the wall of the building. I lie down in the parking lot, stretched out completely. I don't want to go back home. Guillaume mustn't see me in this state. If I go home, it'll mean that I'll have to take off my jewellery and makeup, and have to undress and once again wear skin that doesn't suit me. I want to stay in these clothes for as long as possible. I want to stay in the carefree state that drunkenness allows me to feel. I lie down beside a car under the stars' shameful whispering.

I get back up. Some people tell me they're going to drive me home. I get in their car. I stink of liquor and hops. There's a woman beside me, in the back, and in the passenger seat, in front, there's another man. He hands me a joint that I refuse.

The smell subsists even though all the windows are rolled down. The driver has a radio voice that could put me to sleep if he were to talk for too long. The music assaults my eardrums and I feel the bass's vibration in my bones. It feels like I'm still in the bar. The driver devours me with his eyes in the rear-view mirror. I wonder why his look doesn't cause me to come undone. The heat between my thighs becomes more insistent. I feel like running away and getting lost in his mouth at the same time. I think about Guillaume, who sleeps with closed fists. I get a grip on myself. I won't do anything bad, just have a drink with them and then leave. After several turns, we arrive at his apartment, which is on the third floor. I don't know which neighbourhood I'm in; I didn't pay attention to the road. I suspect that we are in a rich part of Québec City, judging by the luxury cars parked in the courtyard.

Inside, there's dried spaghetti remnants in a pot. A spicy smell makes me turn up my nose. The TV is still on, showing a video game on pause. A fresh autumn breeze passes through an open window and postpones my urge to puke again. I'm going to put my elbows on the ledge and take deep breaths. The others drop their things in the entrance and I turn around to do the same. I throw myself onto the couch with all my weight, no longer able to support my body. It's so soft that if I don't hold on to the sides, I think it might swallow me. I get back up to go to the bathroom before the mirrors break with dawn. Before they take me back to being that filthy, abject, undignified boy. I check to see if there's anything else to drink. My only desire is to sink into my heartbreak. I go back to the couch. It's so tempting to let myself drift away and forget my problems by being engulfed by his silence. I think of Guillaume on the bathroom floor, waiting for me to get out of the shower so we can make love, of his fiery gaze that doesn't light any fires, but rather appeases them. I wish I could be happy with it; it's a strange death to see what you've loved without being able to feel it one last time. My eyelids are heavy. I don't know what time it is. I only know that I'm somewhere between happy and unhappy.

I'm handed some wine. A few minutes later, I can't see anything.

A muffled sound wakes me up. It's my arm hitting the door frame. I'm in someone's arms. They're bringing me to a bedroom, throwing me onto a bed.

The man leans over me, takes off my shoes, and throws them into the corner. He unzips my pants. I can't move a single finger or move my legs. Someone put something in my glass, I'm more than sure. I count myself lucky that I didn't swallow more of the poison; at least I'm conscious.

He lowers my pants and jumps back into the corner of the room. He straddles me. I can't feel his weight, only that I'm out of breath. My penis is there. I don't have a vagina. He searches through my purse until he finds my health card.

"Are you kidding me? It's not your real name, for fuck's sake."

I have no tears, only terror that invades me, that holds back my scream. He keeps slapping me. Blood spurts out of my mouth. He slaps me again. My face reels. I feel nothing. I can only hear the sound of his palms slapping against my skin. His fingernails tear at my thighs. He holds my arms. I feel nothing, at least, on the outside of my body. He spits in my face.

"I'm going to have fun with you anyways."

He turns me around. I start to feel tingling in my face.

I see a pond at twilight.
Birds take flight
    after the firing of a rifle.

An echo persists   in
the forest. It's a   voice, it's
a cry.

My head in the bathwater
so I don't hear Mom   and
Dad   fighting.

In one move, he rips off my wig. This time, I feel my hair being pulled. I stretch out, come back to life or give myself over to death.
His saliva runs
down my face
thick like
lava.

    I start being able to move my limbs a little. He holds me against the mattress. I should think more seriously about death. I think instead of my mom. Of my dad. Of the fact that my mom rarely tells me she loves me. Of the fact that I never say *I love you* to my dad. He hits me again. It feels as though my parents are the ones hitting me.

I can't do anything but have my face shoved in a pillow, anything but know that he is taking pleasure in my suffering.

I would like to talk to him.

To tell him that love exists.

Chilly morning. I get up, not without pain. Autumn touches my body; all I have left is a tank top and underwear. I regain consciousness in a park. A jogger runs by and notices my weak state through a thicket of trees.

"Are you okay? Can I help you?"

Embarrassment, shame. I turn him down.

I take a first step, a groan of pain. His eyes seem to read me like a book.

"I have police contacts if you ever want to file a report."

He holds his hand out, and I get up. He takes a small towel from his backpack and it's sufficient enough to hide my shame. He's wearing blue chrome sunglasses, and looks as though he's looking at me through the sky. He unfolds his towel for me as though he's laying the sheets on a bed before a long sleep. We walk to my place. I feel like I've run a dozen marathons. When I talk, pain reignites my swollen face.

"There's no way I'm going to involve the police."

I never knew speaking could be so laboured. I don't look like much. A dog barks. The buses thrum. Everything is normal; the city doesn't know they're trying to kill its children.

Bruises on my arms, my thighs, my face. It's noon. Curious looks pierce me. The swelling gets worse. It feels like every car that passes wants to steal the last of my dignity.

The man whose name I don't know leaves me at the door to my apartment. The only uplifting part of this is that there are still kind people who want to help others.

I touch my chest, checking for my grandmother's pendant. I find it in seconds at my back, and I'm reassured; it had just gotten turned around. I hold the rose quartz in my hand. I think about my grandma and feel reassured.

I knock on the door. Guillaume opens it after the first knock. He was on alert, waiting, I can see the relief in his face. He has his phone in his hands. Guillaume dissolves into tears. I don't have the strength to cry. I no longer have the strength for anything. He catches me as I'm about to collapse to the ground. He hands me a glass of water. Not without pain, I head to the bathroom. I take a shower, or rather it's the shower that takes me in my exhaustion.

"I'm going to have to go to the hospital," I tell him.

I moan in pain with every touch of the washcloth. Once I'm cleaned and dressed, I join Guillaume, who's waiting to help me get into the car.

Once again, I see the hands of the man who turned me into this, and it brings me back to my own emptiness.

"I knew dressing like that would attract trouble. You wouldn't have gotten your face punched in if you hadn't wanted to draw attention to yourself by dressing like a girl." What he says cuts me in two.

"I don't have time for a lecture. Just take me to the hospital, that's all."

"I'm telling you, it's not good for you."

"I didn't just get punched in the face, Guillaume, I think he raped me too…"

[186]

I raised my voice, which hurts, so I bury myself in my tears. Guillaume stays silent the rest of the drive.

At the hospital, everyone's on edge. The staff don't know how to address me. Is it a woman, is it a man? They see a woman in front of them, but on the health card, there's a man, with the gender marker M, sex: male. I don't have the energy to tell them that I express my femininity through clothing.

Here are my bruises, my cuts. We can talk about my heart and my head another time.

"Fuck, who is it? Who did this to you? Do you remember his address or his neighbourhood at least?"

Seeing Guillaume like this worries me. Try as I might, I can't remember what the man looked like; it's as though he never really had a face. Like a watercolour left outside on a rainy day.

I'm asked if I want to file a police report. I don't see the point since I don't have any details to help find my assailant.

Once in the exam room, I'm asked to take off my clothes. The nurse notices my discomfort. I tell the woman, "I've always felt uncomfortable in my body."

"It's normal after an assault."

I hide my sex with my hands. She has me turn around, examines my bruises.

"Don't you at least remember anything about his car?" Guillaume says impatiently, getting ready to leave the room.

"You can stay, Guillaume. I'd like it if you stayed, please."

He stays, wordlessly, in front of this body transformed by another's hate. The nurse prescribes me pain meds and asks me to come back in a few weeks to take an STI test, as a precaution. As I get dressed, the nurse starts looking through some papers and, at the end of the examination, she passes me a pamphlet about transgender identity and refers me to a psychologist I can talk to about my assault. It's like a revelation. I show the pamphlet to Guillaume, excited.

"Maybe…" he says hesitantly while looking at the floor.

The next day, after having rested, I look up discussion forums. I chat with trans women who live their lives authentically, in broad daylight, and I cry reading their stories. It's been this, all this time, this uneasiness since childhood, this discomfort, this flesh prison that is finally no longer a prison. I was an abandoned house, and now I will be able to live.

Later, Guillaume and I go to Montreal for a consultation. The city burns itself into my retina as I think: this is the island where my salvation lies. I go from total discord within myself to euphoria at having finally understood what troubles me.

"Can we walk a bit before going in?" asks Guillaume. "It's just a lot for me. There's a park right there."

Under the shade of an ash tree, we sit down. His tears fall on their own. I can tell he's trying to hide how nervous he is.

"I will always love you. No matter what's going on with you."

I see myself, young again, in front of that raccoon who I told I was a girl. Did he guard my secret all these years, till the day I was ready for it?

When it's time, I enter the office, full of anxiety. I look at Guillaume before closing the door and, suddenly, I wish that all of this were nothing but the fruits of my imagination.

Guillaume behind a door.

Facing a loss.

The sun streams into the room on this early Montreal afternoon. We hear the clamour of a busy street. Cyclists, pedestrians, drivers, the symphony of a city that never stops. There's laughter from the sidewalk. A truck passes by. The sun makes a halo around the psychiatrist like an apparition from my childhood's illustrated Bible.

No matter what he's going to say in this office, I know I'm ready to hear it. It's a decisive meeting that will have a major effect on the rest of my life. The psychiatrist welcomes me in with a wide smile. He's nothing like what I imagined he'd look like, from talking to him on the phone. He's smaller than me, stocky, with large hairy bear hands. He's wearing a blue shirt, like the ocean, like the sky, like freedom.

"Talk to me about your childhood, how you felt when you were young living in the village, your relationship with your brother, your mother, your father, your relationship to your body."

I speak of how this body, since puberty, has become more and more alien, tell him that I often want to desert it because I don't know how to inhabit it. I tell him I surprise myself by using feminine pronouns, fully at ease, when talking to people who see me the way I see myself. My memories pour out over the hour. The psychiatrist's pen dances as he fills up several pages. With him, I find the words to name the hurricane that cuts through my life: gender dysphoria, characterized by an incompatibility between my sex assigned at birth and my gender identity. Dysphoria has tinged my whole childhood and adolescence with a sadness unnamed until today. He takes me by the hand. He gives me back my sight.

The more I talk about my parents, the more I realize that we've never really been that close, and that it's been an eternity since I've heard from them.

I emerge from the office, empty from sharing all the details. I emerge having lost the weight of a man no longer on my back. Guillaume seems to want to collapse when he learns the news.

We spend the drive back to Québec City on the edge of our seats. I sometimes hear a stifled sob. A sigh. When I try to read him, he shuts down, looks away.

"The landlord called about the new bathtub. We'll finally have something that works properly."

I see right through his attempt at changing the subject. I feel bad for wanting to celebrate the good news. He starts bawling. He has to park on the side of the highway because he can't concentrate properly. His tears pour out. Some disappear in his thick beard as they seek a long-lost warmth. How I wish those tears didn't carry my name.

I share his sadness. It makes me tremble deeply. I kiss him on the cheek. Nothing will be like before. He's losing the man he loved.

A few days later, I quit my job. I can no longer concentrate on my tasks, affected by my assault, the new revelation, and the beginning of the end of our love story. All of this is too much.

I can't get myself out of this lethargy. Since the assault, I have a hard time making it to the corner store. I discuss my feelings about the encounters with my psychiatrist.

Paralysis has assailed me for many days. My psych writes me personally to ask that I come to our sessions. I don't feel like encountering my rapist every time I go there.

My oral health deteriorates rapidly. I'm told that stress is changing the pH levels in my mouth, which is causing cavities. I start to think that my body has decided to digest itself, so that I can disappear once and for all and so that I can stop being a source of discomfort for others. I wake up soaked in sweat in the morning. I have to go to the dentist. It's the season of great floods. I have a sharp pain in my jaw. It's no longer possible to postpone the appointment.

The dentist's office is on the ground floor of an office building. Large full-length windows give onto the boulevard. Inside, everything is very white and bright, blindingly so. Behind a counter riddled with ads for discounts and pricing packages, as well as procedures of all kinds, sits an austere-looking secretary. Her mouth turned down, glasses on the tip of her nose, the phone squeezed between her shoulder and her cheek. I feel a rush of adrenaline. Once she hangs up, I move forward, feeling nauseous. My pain reminds me that I have to talk to her.

I can't get used to the idea that I have to spend at least an hour in a chair, immobile, at the mercy of someone's gaze, someone who will see my face up close. It makes me sad that they will notice the irritation from my shaved beard and stubble while I'm wearing a floral dress. When the time comes, I head to the consultation room. It has the cold, incisive light of a morgue. My hands are clammy. My bangs stick to my forehead. A woman glares at me, and I pretend not to notice. What does she want from me?

I want to scream. To run away as far as possible. It's hard to be at the mercy of all those inquisitive looks. I want to be smooth and unscathed, to show that I'm not dishevelled by the masculinity I've been stifling with a vengeance. I feel dirty under the layers of foundation I've applied, especially for today, when someone will be so close to my face. Dirty fleabag. I'm happy that at least I don't have to show any ID to get dental care. No one suspects that I carry a dead young man in my wallet.

Lying on the chair, my hands placed on my stomach, in prayer. I squeeze my toes when the dentist approaches me. He has a warm voice and a kind face. As long as he doesn't see me, doesn't notice the masculine protrusion under my dress. I'm lying down and I still haven't figured out the right technique to camouflage my crotch.

Against all expectations, there is no question of ambiguity. People aren't always who I think they'll be. Some are well intentioned, like this dentist. Knowing this makes me tear up. I pay my bill with more confidence than when I first came in. I leave the dentist's feeling like something in me has broken open. Another weight lifts from my shoulders. I'm filled with new hope. I start to smile for no one.

The trees are in full bloom; the restaurants are filled to the brim. City life makes me happy, it nourishes me. I go back home. On the sidewalk, my victorious steps sound like my high heels clacking, which I'm wearing in broad daylight.

I can't wait to tell Guillaume about my experience at the dentist's so he can see that I am capable of tiny victories despite my reality. I make the journey home on foot because I still don't feel comfortable getting on a bus and being at the mercy of dozens of stares at once. In any case it's sunny out, and soon it'll also be sunny inside.

While walking by a construction site, five men on a scaffold whistle like kettles ready to spill their hot water. Though at first scared by their reaction, I decide to catch my breath and consider this attention a blessing. The more other men take notice of me, the less Guillaume sees me.

We're in quicksand. Even though I hope I'll make him proud with my victories, the opposite always happens. It pushes him away even further, cuts our conversations short, and he responds to me in monosyllabic answers: yes, no, maybe. Sentences disappear. Sighs take their place. I ask him all sorts of questions like, "Am I pretty?" and "Do you think I look pretty today?" and "What's wrong with you, why aren't you answering me?"

We no longer make love; we unmake it.

Guillaume is always busy during the evenings. I start to see progress, working with my psychiatrist. I no longer associate men with rapists.

I confront the night. Even though I can still remember the cologne he was wearing when it happened, he's not going to rob me of the possibility of making new memories. I won't let him make me more closed off than I already am.

Instead of feeling sorry for myself, I decide to go out to gay bars, where I can express my femininity without being assaulted. When I'm there I know I won't be approached by men who are only interested in my ass. That's where I meet Steph. He's dancing relentlessly on a speaker wearing a small tight-fitting top that reveals his stomach and abs that anyone would die for. Drops of sweat gather on my forehead.

The right side of his head is shaved and tattooed with a snake devouring a cloud. He applies gloss on his luscious lips, which are ready to kiss the world, before explaining to me that he works here. His skin-tight white pants leave nothing to the imagination. He sways his hips to Britney Spears, the Pussycat Dolls. He's a fixture of the night. Everyone knows him or buys him a drink. Everyone wants to be with him. He approaches me.

"Are you looking for your daddy, my sweet girl?" he says in English before paying for my apricot brandy.

This is how he enters my life and helps me pick my head up, despite the sadness in the apartment with Guillaume.

Steph is a drag queen. He's one of this stage's regular performers. Very quickly, we start going out together in the evenings. Most of the time, he's wearing lace-up white boots that go up to his knees. He has as many piercings as the times I've cried in my life. He has angel wings tattooed on his lower back that encircle the word *Daddy* in italics. I'm amazed I met him. Sometimes, he sways his hips on the dance floor in form-fitting dresses, and I call him my eel because of his flexibility and grace.

A week later, we know each other much better. He was born in Ontario, on the shores of a lake he planned to drown himself in when he turned eighteen. We share this desire to plan our own deaths without even knowing that we're doing so. He lives alone in an apartment filled with plants, on the third floor of his depression, with two cats, Henri and Philibert. Henri often sits in a ball on my lap while I listen to Steph tell me his stories. Steph takes Molly in the evenings so he's in shape in case he meets his daddy.

During the day, it's regular Steph, without embellishment, his jaw tinted with a thick stubble, the sign of a heavy beard if he let it grow a few days. The light enters his eyes while he's sitting in his chair, and I notice that they're honey-coloured, a honey I like the second I taste it. While we're talking, I graze my fingers against all the plants in his apartment to remind myself what I've abandoned.

He has this habit of polishing his utensils while

he's preparing lunch, an obsessive-compulsive ritual he cherishes, born of an extraordinary experience as a server in Banff, where he met a man who would play an important role in his life. After he finishes polishing his utensils and setting the table, he makes comforting, soft French toast.

We finish our afternoon lunch by sharing a joint on his balcony, which gives onto a view of his neighbourhood, beneath a tranquil sun. I try not to think too much about going home; I never know what state I'll find Guillaume in, in what state we will both end up.

The more I talk to Steph, the more I realize that I don't know a lot about Guillaume's past and I wonder if we're together for the right reasons or if it's because we mostly don't want to return to being alone.

Steph suggests we go clubbing. It's five o'clock. If I start drinking now, it'll give me enough time to come around to finding myself beautiful before the night flourishes.

But a few hours later, I'll have red eyes, with veins bursting from drinking. I will be told that I look like everyone but myself. Someone will say that he passed me in the copy centre and I'll think back to that girl who didn't know that a guy had a crush on her. I like the idea that it's me he's talking about, that I could look so enticing standing by the photocopier that someone might tell me about it days later. I would like, however, in the deepest part of my being, to experience my beauty without relying on others to show it to me, to live my truth without being ashamed of it. The assault I experienced is always on my mind, but working with my psych helps me through it.

This "him": this island that I have to desert. My psych tells me that I have to stop self-flagellating, to stop making myself responsible for the assault and what happened. I often relive this experience to imagine how I could have acted differently. Being on top of him and beating his face in with my fists. Telling him, you won't have to try to remember my name.

I feel like burning my self-help books. Even if I remind myself every morning that today is a new day, without hate and shame, I don't really believe it, because at the end of this new day, things repeat: *you're tearing apart your relationship, you should be ashamed.* When I have these thoughts, I slap my face. Once, twice, three times, harder and harder, telling myself how much I hate me. I stop when the slaps make me cry. Like when you shake a tree to make its apples fall.

I step out of the bathroom. Steph didn't hear anything because of the loud music vibrating through the carpet. He doesn't know I hit myself, so he compliments me on my blush. He asks where I found such a pretty colour. I feel like telling him I've had this blush ever since I was born.

"Well, are we going out or not?"

I think. Yes, we're going out, Steph, I will have enough time to think about the scum that I am, but it's with tenderness that I will remind myself of the breaths that dig into my neck, a caress down my back that makes me shiver, the light of the streetlamps like the sun's tears showing me the way home. When we get to the bar, I'll get out of the taxi as though being birthed in the hope of a definitive spring. I will remember that I want to be made love to without having to beg for it, that I will ask Guillaume to continue loving this new universe he's discovering, without my feeling guilty for asking. I will ask him how one traverses a field of cacti while being able to live serenely by day and then welcome the night. I will no longer ask everyone if I am beautiful, I will know that I am.

"Hey, is everything okay? You seem a thousand miles away."

Steph brings me back down to earth, and I wake Henri and place him on the floor. He stretches before curling back up into a ball. I envy how easily he exists. I find it touching.

Steph teaches me how to pull up my roots, to live in the moment. I don't know when I'll get out of the thick woods of unending struggle, but while I'm here in this dense incertitude, I learn the names of all the trees and flowers that crop up in my path. I won't have anything to be afraid of because I will have gotten to know them. I'll have learned that they offer me their cool shade and their beauty for free.

Come evening, we go to Steph's bar. I feel like drinking to avoid participating in my love's disappearing act. It's like I'm looking for experiences to convince me that I still care about a world where things keep moving on.

I'm given several drinks. Each shot brings me closer to the origin of my wound and takes me further away from Guillaume. I'm torn. No matter what I do, I can't avoid the inevitable catastrophe. I stop in front of a mirror and don't recognize this woman whose face is disfigured with sadness. It's only when I'm drunk that I can access the person that I've buried. I remove my identity, my gender, my sexuality, I peel back until I reach my dawn. I notice a black mark. If

I dig in the sand, there's a child's scream; I dig deeper and there's a baby already old with its hoarse, blood-curdling cry. I look at it, not knowing if it's me or my baby or maybe just my relationship.

Steph suggests I stop drinking for the rest of the night and brings me a glass of water. The storm is not contained; it's everywhere in me, and it'll take more than one person to put out the fire.

I like the idea of dissolving myself in alcohol faster than an ice cube. I really don't like, however, that the barman refuses to serve me another drink. The taxi driver tells me I'm beautiful like a princess, then adds, "I hope you're kidnapped this evening." I'm so thrown off course that I'm lost for words, and the man continues to stare at me in the rear-view mirror.

"Are you a real woman or trans?" another man asks me in the alleyway.

He's confused. He wants to know why I have a feminine voice and an Adam's apple.

"Do you still have your tool, at least? We could have a lot of fun."

Steph arrives and wrenches me out of his talons.

We head to another gay bar. With Steph, I feel sheltered from cat calls or the harassment of the streets. We dance in the male sweat. I feel my mood shift from the first bar, and become more assured, serene. We laugh. I draw closer to this second brother I have in Steph.

Eurythmics plays, men kiss without worry, love each other, laugh in the rush of inspiring poetry. I tell myself that if I died tonight, it would be in the happiness of being who I am with people who are like me. *Here Comes the Rain Again*. We dance under the rain, while the storm passes. *Talk to me, Guillaume, like lovers do.*

Back at his apartment, Steph suggests we have fries. He stumbles to the kitchen and prepares the rest of our meal. I stumble too, in the joy of this comforting evening. I collide with the furniture. I think of my growing hips, wider since going on hormones, nothing too obvious, but it makes me happy to think that, at night, they expand so a uterus can develop in my belly. We finish the wine we'd left on the table. Steph takes off his sweat-soaked shirt. He's sprawled on the ground, wriggling like an eel. I get down beside him. We watch the ceiling spin. My lips are cracked like a piece of furniture that hasn't been cared for. Steph takes my hand, looks deep into my eyes.

"Don't dive too far into me, you might break your legs."

We break out in laughter. Tears line my smile.

The morning is in flames. I want to live beyond daybreak.

"If you don't do anything, you know that life is going to take charge, right?"

I sigh.

The tears roll down to my ears. I turn away. We're spooning. We breathe like a boat eating the waves. One bite at a time. It's not possible to cut the coming wave with a sword. Better learn to swim into it. To work the current, to not be broken into a thousand pieces.

I feel Steph's breath near me, as if he's trying to warm me up like the donkey or the ox in the nativity scene. I've just been born and I need tenderness. I need heat. My cry pierces the night and will make the sun tremble, tells it, *Hey, you forgot to shine your light over here.* And my life will re-root in love's fertile earth.

We listen to Antony and the Johnsons' "I Fell in Love with a Dead Boy". The record continues its lament and we take comfort in these words, in what dies, in what's born. Again, I think about Guillaume, who I let down once I stopped being the man he fell in love with. Heartache sends me to the bathroom. After puking, I scream. I realize that I'm not who I was expected to be and that I'll always carry the burden of being a surprise, a deception.

"Steph! I'll never be able to carry a child inside me."

"Girl, it's really not that bad. We already have enough work trying to carry ourselves, you beautiful child…"

In an apartment in the Saint-Sauveur neighbourhood, morning opens its eyes, basks a little bit longer in its silky night. Two people with hearts as big as several cities hold hands, one holds the other's hair so that the puke lands with minimal mess while the other empties out all the bad she is doing to herself.

After the intense evening with Steph, I went onto his balcony as he slept like a starfish on the floor. I leaned against the railing. The cold contact of the metal on my back kept me awake. His begonias were suspended in a bloody embrace. They balanced themselves in a latent suicidal pose. Brushing against my hair in the wind, they were reciting psalms to me.

It's summer.
you have to live right now.

A week later, still with Steph, whom I spend more time with than Guillaume.

"Hey, we're looking for new drag queens. Would you be into it? I can see you doing it. You'd be good at it."

Steph hands me an apricot brandy, our ritual drink. The idea resonates strongly within me, as though I were finally learning that Santa Claus is actually real. He can tell I'm no longer with him.

"One of these days, you're going to have to come to terms with leaving Guillaume, if you want to really be happy... I'm telling you this as a friend, girl."

I bury his voice under the techno music, under the tons of shots that pile up. There's no reason to ruin the evening with apocalyptic scenarios. If I can't see the Apocalypse coming, maybe it's because I'm right in the middle of it.

We are the queens of the dance floor. We get there within an hour of the bar opening to warm up the room. Our theatrical gestures fascinate people, who pack together not to dance but to encourage us to continue. I suddenly have an answer to Steph's proposal: yes, I have to perform. The piercing neon-coloured lights showcase how to live our lives with intensity; under their heat, we grimace in pleasure.

People flow in and we put our flaming bodies on display. I'm overflowing with joy. He comes up to me.

Wraps me in his arms. There's no ambiguity between us. A brother and sister under the bar's lasers, in the smoke, in our survival. The waitress offers us shots because we're putting on a show. Steph tells her that I'm interested in doing it professionally.

"Watching you dance, I don't even need to ask you to audition. How about an evening a week to start and then we'll see?"

I don't understand what just happened. It would give me an income while I search for a day job. It would also be a way to continue acting despite the failure of those courses that I abandoned.

"I'm so happy for you, darling. I could even be your backup dancer if you need one!"

We meet up in parks or at his place weekday afternoons to prepare for the Saturday show. I have three songs to perform. I always do a Madonna song; it reminds me of car rides with my dad. Steph introduces me to two of his dancer friends who seem interested in being part of my show. They are muscular but manage to move fluidly. I think, here are some eels in high heels. We laugh. They are like my children, like my brothers, like love, the real kind. The practice sessions go well. I like this happiness I've found through the bar. Steph takes my measurements. He handles the sewing machine like a samurai handles a sword. He makes my costumes. We have fitting sessions until the early hours of the morning, the sands of sleep, one too many drinks down our throats. He is inspired by *commedia dell'arte*. I like the costume he's made me: black and white checks, fitted, with a crinoline; and this Pierrot the Moon mask; or this other one, sparkling with hundreds of jewels he's been sewing on one by one for a week, emerald green, with a high collar and panels on the sides so I can breathe and move with ease. I particularly love the large Swarovski bracelets that look like disco balls when I shake them under the bar lights.

My circle of queer friends expands. I've chosen a new family. It's composed of artists nourishing their eccentric dreams. We want to go on tour throughout Québec. We feel good in the spotlight.

I like coming alive in front of the dressing-room mirrors. The room buzzes like a beehive. Steph sets up my outfits on a clothes rack with wheels. We choke with laughter amidst the clouds of talcum powder. I put on my makeup. I try to recreate the image I have of myself in my head. I superimpose my dreams over my reality. I'm an alchemist. I take back my power.

Guillaume gets home from work, filled with frustration and anger. A cry in his eyes. The man he loves is dying. I feel helpless but I have butterflies in my stomach at the thought of how alive I will be on stage. The stage gives me strength to get up in the morning.

"You always turn the apartment upside down with your things."

It's true that I could make more of an effort. I have a tendency to scatter myself in the joy of inner fireworks. I pick up powders, makeup brushes, sponges, and jewellery.

"It's become a total mess ever since you started your shows…"

"And yet it's in this mess that my life gains meaning."

Heavy silence. The apartment seems to want to explode. I go all in.

"Would you like to come see my show sometime?"

His jaw tenses. I understand.

I won't insist.

In between his tight lips slides an "I love you" on an iron wire.

Steph, the dancers, and I sit around a table, drinking a bottle of wine before the show. I've made some noodles. We don't usually eat much before the show. We head to the bar in Steph's car. The city streams past, and it's like it's entering me. I become the city, with all of its effervescence, its risks, its chaos, its dreams.

Once we're ready, wigs placed, high heels laced, garters on, once we're ornamented like charms, Steph brings me my cellphone from where I'd left it near the oven. There's a text from Guillaume:

I can't anymore. It's your sequins or me.
If you do your show today, it's over.

My face turns white.

"Who is it, darling?" asks Steph.

I don't say anything because I don't want to ruin the joyful atmosphere that's been present since the beginning of supper. I try to line up my steps, to go straight ahead, but if I go forward, I'll be heading towards my downfall.

From the dressing room, we can hear the shouts of a frenzied crowd. It will be our turn soon. I finish zipping up my Lycra one-piece. Steph is already by the backstage exit. My expression is vacant.

"Qué pasa, bella?"

Having formed the habit in childhood of not saying anything when something is wrong, I settle for pasting a smile on my face. I feel like dropping everything. Like pretending I'm feeling nauseous so I can shrink away like when I was in gym class.

They announce the name of our group. I take Steph's hand.

"Hold me tight. I'm going to need it."

Steph doesn't really understand what's going on, but he holds me tight. We're behind the curtain. After having grown up with parents like mine, I tell myself it's not love if it's a threat.

The curtain rises. The music starts, and an uncommon and thrilling clamour fills us with happiness.

The crowd doesn't know it, but they are clapping for a woman who is holding herself up.

*G*uillaume couldn't come to terms with the fact that I decided to get up on stage despite his threat. He no longer speaks to me. His moods tire me. The sun barely rises before I'm exhausted by the day. My anxiety emerges and becomes more and more incapacitating. I have to remind myself to breathe multiple times a day.

Hormone therapy really affects my energy. I have a hard time getting used to it; I experience nausea on top of nausea on top of vertigo. It's still nothing compared to the suffering of not being myself.

Despite the fatigue weighing down my limbs, I still manage to get to my neighbourhood health centre, CLSC. It's early. Stores are just starting to get busy. It's my favourite part of the day: the wildness of the night giving way to morning. The neighbourhood is, for a few moments, an expanse of smooth water.

I walk into the CLSC without taking off my sunglasses. There's no way I'm going to let anyone detect a single sign of nervousness in my gaze, frantic and jetting everywhere. I take out the papers for the blood test from my bag. My endocrinologist asked me to go take some tests to make sure that my body is properly integrating the hormones. The woman at the reception doesn't bat an eye. I hand her my health card.

"The name that's written on the card isn't the right one," I tell her.

And I explain my situation to her. I tremble in fear that she might think I'm a weirdo. It makes sweat beads collect in my armpits. I shift my weight every two seconds. I'm out of breath. How do I properly measure out my voice? It has to be loud enough to pass through the partition in the window but low enough so that the people in the waiting room don't hear me.

I take off my glasses. A man stares at me over his magazine. I wonder if it's because he finds me pretty or strange. I inhale deeply and exhale out of my nostrils to calm myself.

Humanity's beauty reveals itself that morning: a head resting on a shoulder, a kid who wanders around in his youthful wonder despite his fever, a woman who looks at her lover as though she just met him.

The thing I'm dreading the most happens. My masculine name resonates through the intercom. I don't dare get up. I hope they'll think this guy just didn't show up to his appointment and that they'll call someone else. But because I need these blood tests for my endocrinologist, I don't have the option of leaving. The man from before shoots me an inquisitive look. I am up, paralyzed by shame.

Once I'm alone with the nurse, she does the blood test. She doesn't seem to make a connection between my masculine name and the person sitting beside her. She thinks I'm pregnant and it's a routine test. I smile to myself.

Yes, I am pregnant with myself.

It's a very grey day. Rain drums against the metal of the cars as I tally up all the things I have to replace. A collection of CDs I broke under Steph's watchful eye at the end of a party. Guillaume's guitar, demolished in a fit of anger. An aquarium, because the glass cracked just like our relationship.

All this violence written in a notebook, hidden in the back of a drawer, like you wish you could do with your memory.

I listen to Barbara's "Dis, quand reviendras-tu?" on repeat. I sing it to Guillaume, hoping it will help me get back into his good graces. His body doesn't react to my shape nor the softness of my skin. In fact, I feel like it repulses him. My skin has become too soft on hormones. I still hate who I am, but now for another reason. I'm losing the one I love. I drink up the sweet talk from men who try to woo me. I drink a lot of rum with no ice.

The mornings rise without my noticing. I drift in uncertainty. I float in murky waters. It seems like no matter what I do, I'll end up a loser. I shower several times a day, look at myself in the mirror, inspect myself. The hormones have visible effects. My breasts grow a little, nothing particularly noticeable. It hurts me. It makes me smile. A second adolescence, bordered this time with the right person's tears. My smile dims when I see Guillaume. That day, before getting into the shower, I grab my scissors and cut off the hair that I've been growing for several months. It was the first time I had had shoulder length hair.

Snip snip.
Snip of the scissors.
Strike of the hammer.
The floor is carpeted with shame.
Tears devour my weeks and months of feminization.

Oh look, I'm a handsome little boy; it's what is expected of me. You've been served. All you have to do now is devour me, until there's nothing left. A rotting carcass.

I cry.

I wait for the storm to pass so I can leave the bathroom. I mask my face with sordid cheer. Guillaume is in the kitchen, preparing his lunch. He turns around when he hears me coming and, when he swallows, the food goes down the wrong way. It's like he's seen death.

On the bus, with giant tinted windows, my head is filled with everything I don't say to Guillaume, of what I'm thinking and re-thinking, of what I keep quiet instead of screaming out. More and more, I start forgetting to eat. I think about the drag shows I'm still doing, but the passion is no longer there. Each show is like stabbing Guillaume. The landscape splits in two with each of my cries. I look at the girl in the seat in front of me with her long, blonde mane of hair. I would love to cut it off and wear it on my head like a tiara.

In the course of that year, friends, poets mostly, enter my life. My first poetry event takes place in the house of a woman who gives a five-hour performance. She's in a white tank top and tiny panties. She's right in the middle of the living room. The people around her sometimes look at her, and sometimes don't. She just stands like that, without drinking or eating, barely blinking. She's invisible in the crowd. There's a low table in front of her. The lamp's lighting imitates a candelabra and turns her skin golden. There's a black Sharpie on the table. People are told to write what they think of her on her skin, to show how much we carry others' judgments; they follow us wherever we go. I've never been able to erase my Sharpie stains; the ink that they've poured from their mouths at school will stay with me till after I'm dead.

I'm excited at the idea of meeting new people. This time, I'm myself, a woman taking back her life. I want to get to know myself better. It's the point in my life when I abandon, for a time, books in favour of human stories, the novels that are my poet friends, with their lives as extraordinary as my own. The woman's arms are now entirely covered in writing that is almost indelible, like dazibao posters. Someone takes off her tank top. Another writes "You need to lose yourself before you can find yourself" on her collarbone.

Gorged and drunk on poetry, I stumble into the house's massive corridor, which is filled with antique decorations. It's like being in a Virginia Woolf novel. The French doors open onto a small group, animatedly talking about poetry in the public space. Another door leads onto a garden where several poets from the city are sitting around a fire, hypnotized by the flames and frantically gobbling toasted marshmallows. Some dance to the beat emerging from a small speaker placed on a wicker chair. Bordering the garden, there's lush vegetation that reminds me how much I miss the countryside, particularly the river and afternoons at the beach. So many tides now separate me from my mom, whom I ran away from in my sands of unease. I thank these trees for bringing me some sense of hope. I know one day I'll find the words; they're written somewhere in the silence.

I hesitate between sitting down with people around the fire or simply walking from one heady discussion to another. We talk about Plato, about Judith Butler and her gender theory. I didn't think it was possible for me to feel good outside my relationship with Guillaume, which is on its last legs. I even allow myself to get pulled into superficial discussions; it allows me to take a break before joining another animated conversation. I can no longer tell which one of us went rotten first. I don't know how endings start, and how much time it takes to drag out a long, anguished one. I don't know when we stop breathing, how much time it takes before the brain understands that there's nothing left for it in life anymore.

I climb the steps of a swaying staircase in order to get

to the bathroom. The vague smell of urine hovers in the air. It's like being at a music festival. A line snakes along the hallway and down to the last step at the bottom. I have a short skirt on and, when I go up each step, I secretly hope that people are imagining the fun things that could happen tonight.

I sit on the bed in one of the bedrooms, or rather I let myself fall onto it. My legs are all pins and needles. The skylight lets in the faint light of a streetlamp and the beginning of the blue hour. This blue makes me melancholy. I realize that I dread the night, but when she leaves, I understand that I loved her.

A man comes over and sits beside me on the bed. He strokes his pants with his tattooed hands. He has an emerald-green silk jacket—like Guillaume's eyes. He seems nervous. He reminds me of myself, and how I always feel like too much or not enough. "I was never enough during my childhood," I tell him.

"But you were something," he responds.

We play around with this philosophy and time passes without us noticing. His hands approach me until it's my thighs that are tattooed. I now have an open bird cage, and a fox looking at it. He notices that I look puzzled and he pulls his hands away.

"Sorry," he says, "I should have asked before. I wanted to tell you that even though it's the first time we're talking, I see you, and you're inspiring."

He knows what to say to make me feel good. This is the first time since I don't know when that someone is this soft with me.

Some people come to talk to him. From his hooked nose, I guess he might be Greek. His eyes are big and open, as large as his smile. I think again about Guillaume and me, who no longer smile, who always look like we're going to a funeral. I don't know how long we're going to celebrate the dead body of our love. When was the last time Guillaume smiled? It's nothing more than an image. It's nothing more than a sound.

I get up at the same time as him.

"You're beautiful," he tells me.

I stroke my short hair.

"You think? Even with my hair like this?"

"Yes."

You're beautiful. These words that I've sought so often from Guillaume's mouth, look how they come out all by themselves from elsewhere, from the mouth of another. I feel like kissing him on the mouth but, finally, my lips land on his cheek to thank him.

"Frédéric, it was a pleasure meeting you."

I need to get myself out of this situation before it escalates; if not, I'll be in trouble. Excusing myself as I pass by him, I hit the wall with my back, and a hanging canvas falls on my head and slides to the ground. It's a painting of a sailboat in the middle of the sea. We burst out laughing.

"It must mean you're ready for a trip," he says, his voice gruff from cigarettes and alcohol.

I feel like escaping on a boat with him. The evening ends, and every visible inch of the performer's body is covered in marker lines. I haven't written anything on her and, as it stands, I no longer know how to express myself.

I return to my bed. Guillaume is asleep. I don't close my eyes, even though fatigue weighs me down. I think back to the man's words, *You're beautiful*, of flowers growing despite the snow. The meeting in that house marks the beginning of several new encounters across the following weeks. The birds are waking up and I spend nights drinking, celebrating, locked in embraces. There's an emerald-green flicker that wanders, I don't know where to, but its light helps keep my eyes open. Behind my eyelids, there are too many images I don't want to see. I see Guillaume leaving our love in each item of his clothing. I see all the possibilities of his leaving, the different moods, the different expressions. Could we be the exception and leave each other with smiles on our lips, like when you leave the gym after sweating your life away?

I think of all the radiant faces that I leave behind when I go back home. We return to our dysfunctional relationships and remember evenings like these to help us find the courage to continue our struggle.

During dance practice for one of our upcoming shows, Steph notices my short hair. "You don't love yourself enough, eh…? Lucky for you, I went wig shopping last week."

I invite my poet friends to come see my show. Before I head to the bar, Guillaume blocks my way.

"I don't know who this woman is that you're trying to be. I don't know what you're playing at."

"For the first time in my life, Guillaume, I'm not playing."

Frédéric once again wears his emerald-green jacket, and he always has a big smile when he sees me. I blush beneath his gaze. I think about Guillaume. The fateful moment of our goodbye.

After the show, we go get some air on the patio. We share a pitcher. Our mouths touch through the imprints we leave on the glass. I'm fifteen again.

I get home from the bar, dripping with sweat yet again. I place my earrings and my rings on my bedside table. The clinking in the porcelain dish reminds me I live a double life. Guillaume sleeps with closed fists, which softens him. The only time we can coexist peacefully is when he sleeps.

That exhausting moment happens again, where I try to get back into a boy's suit to try and please him. My radiant face disappears bit by bit as I use makeup wipes. Exhausted, I fall on the bed, asking myself how it's possible to fall in love with sadness.

I don't dare imagine what I might have become if Guillaume hadn't gotten me out of the countryside. I don't think I would have been able to continue living. I would have either died, devoured by wolves, or hung at the end of a rope like a pendulum marking the strokes of absence.

Despite all of our recent tension, I have to admit that he's done a lot for us. The fact that I'm unemployed right now, while waiting to change my first name, makes me ill tempered. From day to day, I feel like I'm heavy in debt, in silence, in neurosis.

Tonight, I screamed into the blankets because I didn't want to bite my cheeks and also because I didn't want the little kid playing happily in the parking lot to hear the awful pain I experience being alive.

It's winter, and today I head to a café to work on a poetry piece with my artist friends. We each have our areas of interest. One person draws, another paints, and I write poems inspired by their work. The smell of floral incense floats through the café. I think about Guillaume and how he hasn't said "I love you" in a very long time. I try to chase this image, to tell myself that if he didn't love me, we wouldn't be living together. Guillaume went over to a friend's to write some music. When he used to devote himself to his art in my presence, he would smoke a joint, come over to kiss me, and then go back into his music. I miss his body on mine.

Even though I hate winter, I find reasons to go out. I organize impromptu meetings in cafés with Steph and the dancers, or with my poet friends. Steph worries about my mental and physical health.

"You're only holding yourself up on two little sticks right now. You should never let yourself waste away for a man, no matter how hot he is."

Steph makes me stews, sandwiches.

Yesterday, I slid under the sheets to warm myself, my body, and my heart. I wrapped Guillaume in between my thighs. He drew himself from my embrace and turned his back to me. I force myself to eat. I force myself to puke. I no longer feel like forcing myself to love a wall.

One day, my meeting with my friends finishes earlier than expected, so I decide to go see Guillaume at his composer friend's studio, a few streets away. The glacial air sticks in my nostrils. A man in a parking lot clears the snow off his car; today, I sweep away my doubts, my anxieties, and I appreciate life.

I ask the building's receptionist where the studio is. After a labyrinth of hallways, I find the door. I can't wait to see the surprise on Guillaume's face.

I stop dead. My heart beats loudly. Guillaume is kissing a man. He doesn't notice my presence. He has everything I don't have: a beard, muscles, strong hands. I'm stupefied. Guillaume finally notices me and pulls back from the embrace.

I am both disturbed and stunned by this spectacle, their devouring, and the way it makes me disappear.

He clings to the wall to regain his senses and offers me a nervous smile to try and make amends. He pulls himself together, as though tomorrow the sky will still be the same colour.

He approaches for a hug.

"I'm sorry," he dares say to me.

He reeks of pot. His face whips sideways. I slapped him so fast and hard; I don't understand why there's blood on the carpet. A stream of blood on his lips, his chin.

I leave the studio in a fury. The heavy snow melts on my burning face even as my tears freeze. I walk through Old Québec where the stores and apartment buildings are on the verge of collapse. My boots fill with water. Under the Saint-Jean Gate, I take a second to regain my breath and crouch down. The city is atomizing into a black hole. I feel like the world is rejecting me. I return to my apartment and urgently pack my suitcases. I shiver, a fever snaking through me since I witnessed that incongruous scene.

In our absence, our apartment has become an icebox. A white mount has formed on our stove. A shining snow that makes me think of a heap of diamonds. I try to chase it away with my hands. To chase everything that is trying to overtake me. The night, the rain, Guillaume's smiles are no longer for me.

My rage fogs up the window. There's a broken shard of plate in my hand. I open myself. A little. A lot. Deeply. My wrist trembles but the skin splits like paper.

Guillaume arrives while I'm giving myself a third cut. With lightning speed, he grabs a cloth and applies it to my arm and gets rid of the piece of plate with his other hand. I'm discombobulated; today the world doesn't want me dead.

I can't speak, nor hear anything at all. I press against him as he puts my jacket on. I have a photo of Pénélope, my childhood doll, in my hands. During disasters, people often bring the things that are most precious to them before leaving their house to its fate. I want my childhood to hold my hand.

We go outside together. He helps me into the car and we head to the hospital. I stop bleeding. By the time we arrive at the reception, I'm seeing double. It's hard to support my own weight. Noticing my condition, the staff take charge of me right away. The receptionist gives Guillaume a form to fill out and asks me to sign after, to authorize them to commit me given my psychological distress.

Face swollen with tears. The receptionist takes notes. Guillaume touches my forehead, ruffling my bangs. Now that my forehead has been discovered, I feel like they'll be able to read my thoughts. It makes me panic so bad I scream.

An orderly tells me to follow him. I spit on his face. Guillaume shrinks at the end of the hallway; I hear his cries in between my shouting. At that moment, two paramedics push a stretcher into the hallway and I lose sight of him.

Four concrete walls muffle the sounds. In this room, they wait for people to fade away and forget their dreams. I no longer know why I'm here. In this room, the sun and the moon follow each other without us being able to see. I am dangerous. The nurse calls me by my masculine first name.

"I'm begging you, don't call me that!"

They assign me a room the next day. My neighbour is a girl who is staring at the cover of a book. She doesn't notice when I arrive. She has a brown braid which she plays with all the time. I feel strange in this sterilized space.

My neighbour sings children's nursery rhymes every night. Lying with her head down where her feet should be, her smile looks like a grimace. I want her to tell me what life is like backwards. Perhaps, that's the way back to our mothers' wombs. Though she was cold with me, my mom's love is the only thing I never want to get away from.

I get a call from my mom the next day, and I think about coincidences, about what is dreamed in secret.

"Guillaume told me everything… All of this makes a lot of sense… But you're still my boy."

My mom's voice trembles, and I'm too far away to brush away her tears.

"I know you'll always think of me as a boy, but can I at least be your daughter?"

"It won't be easy, my b—… my girl, but I'm here, if you need money or anything."

Mom cries. These floods that she's feared ever since we were young, I think it's because she held them all in.

I spend most of my days playing chess with a guy called Benjamin who also got hospitalized for trying to commit suicide. It's his fourth time. I don't know if it's because our scars look the same, but we become friends. Our injuries bring us together.

I lose most of the time and, if I win, I know it's because he leaves me openings. His steel-blue eyes can think two or three moves ahead. He takes his time, digs through his red beard for a strategy.

Our dinner arrives. We sit side by side in our gowns. He gives me the rest of his food because he doesn't like oatmeal. Our walks through the courtyard behind the hospital render me euphoric. I don't know if it's the medication, or just the joy of no longer having to think about anything for the first time in my life.

Guillaume visits me once, no longer knowing what to call me. We don't speak.

We watch each other.

We inspect each other.

We wonder whether maybe there's still a little morsel of love beneath the hate.

"I just don't know how to deal with all of this… It's hard for me too. I really thought you were going to die."

When I look at Guillaume, I can't help but see his mouth pressed against that man's.

"It doesn't justify what happened in the studio."

We're silent until the end of the visit.

"I love the boy that you are, but I can't wrap my head around the girl you're becoming."

And I respond between clenched teeth, "Don't come back. There's no point. I'm done grieving for us."

Guillaume doesn't turn around when I say this. It doesn't hurt me either, because for months now I've gotten used to him turning his back to me.

In the evening, I look at the stars from my small window. The girl next door doesn't snore. It's a change from Guillaume. The day I leave the hospital, Benjamin seems sad.

"If you come back, I mean I don't wish that for you, you know, eh, it would suck, it would mean that you aren't doing better, but anyways, I want to say, if you end up coming back, would you count the stars on my face?" he asks me while pointing to his freckles.

"Yes, for sure."

"I can't wait to go to Montreal, for my new life, I can see that if I want things to change, I have to do things differently to get different results. Thank you for all the chess matches."

At the moment of separation, we embrace. I notice he's tearing up. I gather his face in my hands and thank him. "No contact," shouts an orderly.

Guillaume waits for me at the hospital exit, leaning against his car, looking off into space. I pray that it'll pass but in my heart I know we're over. It's him or me; it's not even a question. No matter what we choose, winter will be longer for us.

Guillaume is more patient with me. My time at the hospital seems to have made him more aware of my suffering. I sleep on the couch; there's no way I'll go back to sleeping with him. I don't know the whole story, whether it was the first time or if he has a habit of kissing other guys. I don't want to rub salt into my wound.

Despite everything, I notice the effects of hormone therapy. Everyone sees different results. For me, my butt gains some shape, my hips widen, my breasts are growing and they hurt.

My male skin sloughs off; it's the snake's moulting season. I can finally stand to look at myself in the mirror. This is my body, delivered to me. It's the only thing keeping me alive.

I'm not interested in getting back on stage. Steph expresses his disappointment, but he also understands. I spend more and more time with him. We sip our tea and discuss the collapse of my relationship from every angle. My grandmother calls me every week—she has gotten into the habit of calling ever since finding out she almost lost me this winter.

It's inevitable. The official breakup is mutual, but it's an agreement that is more like a resignation, a resignation to amputate a gangrenous arm so as not to die. While sipping tea, Steph helps me look for an apartment on the Internet. I carry a cargo of tears, and my body trembles uncontrollably. I think about Montreal. I have to be in another city to avoid the madness I'm being thrown into because of this separation.

During a walk in the Sainte-Catherine-de-la-Jacques-Cartier woods, Guillaume and I come across the carcass of a stray cat, missing its head. We look at each other in front of the decapitated body, stunned. This idea of the living having lived, and no longer existing. It makes me think of us. Later, Guillaume looks me straight in the eye for the last time.

"I will always love you."

He starts crying. I wipe his tears.

This sadness goes right through me. It no longer lingers in my heart. That evening, I cry until my sides hurt.

Guillaume asks me to stay a boy until I leave "… so I have a nice memory of you." I acquiesce while clenching my teeth. When he sees me "dressed as a woman," it erases the image of the boy he fell in love with. Because I know I'm leaving next summer no matter what happens, it doesn't bother me; at least, that's what I tell myself.

In the spring, bars become my home. I stay until closing time so I can dress in the clothes I want for as long as possible: dresses, tank tops, skin-tight jeans, high heels. In the greatest of silences, I get ready at the apartment to emerge at night, renewed by this city. Men hit on me, offer me drinks. The time to go home always comes too quickly. Bitterly, I watch my makeup disappear down the sink's drain.

. The tension is palpable. Guillaume and I fight more and more. Shatter flowerpots and our voices. When it's nighttime, we tense against the uncertainty, the reason for our next argument.

Guillaume throws parties at the apartment without asking. Sometimes I arrive home as drunk as he is. We meet at the precise point of our common pain. We stare at each other. We bark louder than the dogs.

One day, I decide to bury the hatchet and stay for one of his parties. There are tons of people in all the rooms. I try to find somewhere to sit, but there are even three people talking on the bed. I understand Guillaume; he tried to find some comfort, some love, in the man he kissed. He laughs loudly with his guests. I will no longer be the one making him laugh.

Instead of feeling trapped in this whirlwind of an evening, I decide to take charge of pouring shots. I can no longer understand the conversations amidst the exciting shouts of the party. I don't know what we're celebrating but I take advantage, getting outrageously drunk by drinking all the different kinds of alcohol everyone brought.

I end the night in a pool of my own puke, on the bathroom floor. Guillaume helps me get up.

That evening is the last time he does that.

Slumped on the ground after another argument, we watch each other crying for a bit. We no longer recognize one another through our scowls. It's like all the beauty of what we've experienced together dwells there— our laughter, our bursts of joy. And yet, none of that keeps us from fighting.

We envy couples who walk around with smiles on their faces. We now live together with knots in our stomachs.

I live at Steph's while waiting to move cities. I go see my grandmother for an important event. She has shrunk and her back is curved under the weight of her years but she still continues to wear lipstick and a touch of makeup. A rose that will never wilt.

"You kept your pendant all this time. It makes me proud, my girl."

It's the season of intoxicating floral smells. She's wearing her lavender jacket and a matching skirt. I'm holding her hand, but she's also holding mine.

Together, we steady each other. She's lost weight and I'm worried she'll topple over from the slightest gust of wind. We pass by the Japanese lilacs that have decorated the front of her house since my childhood. She's still delighted by their immaculate whiteness, and each time she passes them, she pauses to breathe them in.

"People who don't stop to appreciate what life has offered them won't remember anything when they're about to die."

I take this reflection very seriously.

A man sitting on a bench gives her an appraising look.

"Alright, it's starting again," she sighs. "When will they understand that I will never love anyone other than your grandfather? He was the one and only."

She takes my arm, takes tiny steps, and I slow down to match her pace, to appreciate the view. My grandmother is a happy tortoise.

At the office of the Directeur de l'Etat Civil, a officer recites legal oaths. Since I need a witness for the swearing-in, I thought of my grandmother right away, because she understands what I am going through. When I told her that I was a woman, she said, "Finally, you've opened your eyes." I was touched by her reaction.

My birth ritual. Soon, I will receive a new birth certificate with the first name I chose as well as a new gender marker going from male to female. Grandma's smile is stamped on her face. She brightens the day. We're elated to take another step towards my new life.

When we get back to her place, she sits on the balcony that looks out onto the backyard, our favourite spot for talking. I carry bowls of yogurt which we'll garnish with nuts. I open the fridge. On the door shelf, I notice floor cleaner. Out of curiosity, or maybe fear, I check under the sink. The soy milk is sitting beside the garbage bin.

I have to prepare myself for the possibility that she might not remember me one day.

I think back to the heaviness of living with Guillaume. It would be easier if I could hate him. How can I turn against the person who gave me back my light?

I have to move as soon as possible. Change cities. It's not conceivable to haunt the places, the neighbourhoods, the alleyways of a lost love. I have to move. To get farther away from the place where I felt my first heartbeat.

As the end of our relationship approaches, I come up with the idea of organizing a farewell trip in order to honour the years I spent with Guillaume. We drive to New Brunswick. Armed with music and bags of chips, we set off on the road heading for our goodbye. Each song that plays is about us. The kilometres coil around my neurosis, hold me until I'm at peace: these are my last moments with him. I manage to sleep along the bumpy route, which rocks me like my mom.

During the trip, I'm finally recognized for the woman that I am. At the Bay of Fundy, we scour the seashore in search of rocks. One in particular catches my attention. It's shaped like an egg. Everything I see reminds me of my rebirth.

At the inn, we ask for a room with two beds.

When we get to Québec City, I head back to Steph's, which is where I'll stay until I move. I see Guillaume one last time to say our goodbyes. We hug for an eternity.

My memory doesn't want to get rid of the scent of our first meeting. Guillaume smells like a rose and I remember my small body, like an injured bird, against his chest one evening in his basement.

"Have a good life, beautiful."

First night without Guillaume. I feel like dying. To say that a life wants to die gives me vertigo. I will organize my death the way people plan a wedding, not forgetting any of the details. I am nothing without him.

I'd be curious to see what my skin would look like in the seconds following my death, in the hours before I'm found. The blue of my veins coming to the surface on the way to the morgue. I feel like numbing myself, like my mom after getting hit, like my dad after a beer. I want to die naked, without any special clothing for my grand departure, naked, the same as I entered the world.

Hochelaga. The neighbourhood where I start my new life. My apartment is by a primary school where kids play in the schoolyard. A little girl is looking over the fence. I smile at her when I catch her eye. We recognize each other.

Steph was the one who found this furnished two-bedroom. Around a pizza, Steph cries in my arms. Emotions are peaking. We go out to a bar downtown at the end of the day. I see everything with new eyes. I need new people, I need things to move as much as possible, so I don't think about Guillaume too much.

I have to find a job in Montreal. I settle into city life and hope that that this place has enough room for my overflowing heart. The buildings grow like weeds. With tracing paper, I try to transpose the forest from my childhood onto this to-be-discovered city. I float, re-vitalized. I find my lightness again.

I pay attention to my new environment. The apart-ment's sounds are new sounds that take getting used to. I bathe my face in dawn's light in order to relive the high tides and the hurricanes, to understand them. This sun is not the same one that rose in the countryside years ago, in my childhood. I sometimes jump when the floorboards creak or when the old heating pipes act up. In this apartment, I can hear the muffled murmur of cars, they buzz with the sound of life beginning. Yes, the light is different in this small space: it finally reaches things.

The ash tree near my window protects me from the ugliness of the world. Children's laughter cuts through the branches. One time, I spend a whole afternoon watching the tree sway in the wind; it reminds me of the trees in the woods where I grew up. It's already been several days, despite the crying, despite the weight loss. Who are you becoming, Guillaume? Who watches over your nights now?

The mattress I bought online unfurls like a Swiss roll. It's where I'll live from now on and, until further notice, spend my nights. This mattress placed directly on the floor will be the raft I ride upon the swells of days. I sleep with two or three books on my bed. I latch onto certain passages like little buoys of hope that help me navigate uncharted waters.

I talk to Steph every day. He's worried that I'll take my life. He promises that Québec isn't the same since I left. I have trouble remembering the names and faces of my poet friends. I ingest alcohol in industrial quantities and it robs me of my memories.

Sometimes, I see faces that I don't know and memories that have never happened. Repressed desires. From some-where else. I can't stay in one place. Maybe I'll never put down roots and that will be my destiny? Why is it a question of inevitability? Why am I talking as though I've seen everything of life?

A path through the woods, the mud, the storm, naked feet sliding in sandals. Hoping for the arrival of a white caribou like a new beginning. This beach and the sea's song. Do you remember, you were throwing stones into the depths of the river's gorge. It swallowed your dreams and spread opportunities for growth along its coastline.

What I lived with Guillaume is fleeting and it slips through my hands like a salmon returning to the place of its birth. I should have made the most of it while it was happening, I tell myself. My grandmother and I call each other often. I feed this fear that she no longer knows who I am. I tell myself that, at least, I know a bit more of who I am.

I think back to that evening at my grandmother's, like a hand covering a child's eyes to try to stop her from growing up too quickly. But the plants' lustre brings me back to the light from the streetlamps, which has grown in an illogical way, near a lilac that has not asked for anything.

I jerk awake at night, paralyzed by the size of my mattress. I adopt a small Calico cat that sleeps with me and jumps when I wake up. She sleeps on my chest and purrs, she rubs her head against mine, a mom's hand for a feverish child.

Sometimes, for several days, I can't feel the water from the shower on my skin and I have no more tears. I do my best so that my cries don't go through the thin plaster walls and worry my neighbours. Sometimes I smother myself with my pillow right until I'm about to fall asleep; sometimes I cry out and nothing comes out of my throat. Even my cry is exhausted.

Everything drains me, empties me.

I am porous.

I am almost.

I hold a picture of me as a kid in my hands. This tiny tot who will later be assaulted, intimidated, frequently betrayed, who will ask what's the point of dreaming if she'll always be let down. And I tell her that I love her. That even if I'm in pain, I love her. I need to stay in this raw feeling, like charcoal. It's only at the end that the diamond shines through, that we can see through it. The diamond is forever charcoal. Don't forget this.

I try my best to hold on to the beauty of the world under the guidance of a therapist who helps me manage my anxiety. I grieve in order to get rid of the memory of my rape. It collects dust, and is always there, in the back of the room. I come out of the consultation office feeling like I have been stripped of my skin and that everyone can see my muscles and nerves, which have been contracting in sadness since childhood.

Sometimes, a passerby will make small talk with me on the way back home and I won't feel like running away like before. Sometimes, it's this trick of the light, near the end of the afternoon, that heats the cars' sheet metal and that dazzles me, so I have to stop. I take advantage and fill my lungs with fresh air. Sometimes, it happens to be when it snows in full sunlight or when the drops of water from the thaw welcome laughter and the reckless feet of children. The weeks pass with shocking speed and I stay here, longing with desire to experience the beauty of life.

I'm starting to get used to my neighbourhood. I say hello to the workers at the market and greet them by their first names; they know what I'm going to order before I even open my mouth. I buy fruit, make salads for myself, my taste buds finally tasting something.

The time comes to get rid of my facial hair, to clear the bramble that covers my armpits. I remember the first hairs on my torso and the speed with which I plucked them out one by one.

A woman shaves her face each day with a trembling chin.

A woman cuts her face several times hoping that, one day, the hairs will not grow back.

A woman fights a hydra.

A woman closes her curtains to be sure that her crying doesn't make its way onto the street.

At the aesthetician's, the hairs burn under the laser and leave behind a trail of smoke. It makes me think of all the times I wanted to pluck myself out by the roots.

In my free time, I meet men, far too many to write about in my journal.

It's excruciating to miss someone when you still have so much to discover in yourself. These people that place all their weight on me without worrying about my ribs cracking; I love them and hate them. I turn on the oven fan and the noises from the alleyway fill my apartment as though I were outside. When morning comes, I never know how to open my eyes.

We understand each other in our sadness. Our stories cut short when I start feeling attached; when I get attached, it's to men as unfeeling as cinder blocks.

But when people take the time to listen, I feel understood. I give my body and soul to those who don't care for the latter, and yet, I learn. They are custom-built homes for me.

The insomnia that torments us has no reason for the ephemeral happiness that we experience at each of our encounters. All that matters to me is being loved as a woman. Some people want to know me as I am. They want to love me as I am.

Once, I had sex with a man whose apartment is haunted. He warns me right from the get-go, when we begin spending time together. I start talking to his ghost. I need love so badly that I get used to this ethereal presence. The ghost has short blond hair, a beard, he's wearing a jacket and has dark circles under his eyes. We recognize each other as two people who half exist. I tell the guy that I know how to speak to ghosts since I've been one my whole life.

He's excited because I brought wine. I think that the quality of the wine is proportional to the quality of the hopes we feed into this date. And so, my love is a dépanneur. Sometimes, when I straddle him, I feel like I'm being watched from behind, but I stay where I am. I need to feel him inside me since it's killing me not to feel myself. I think about that presence. I like that I'm being looked at from both sides, to remind me that I have depth, that I'm not just an image.

It's a summer of bicycle lanes and poetry under the trees in Parc Lafontaine. A summer of joints rolled between fingers filled with desire for each other. I think about all these tiny mouths at the end of my fingers. My hair sticks to my forehead with the same tenacity with which I stick to men. I put my hair up in a ponytail even though I know that when my throat is exposed like this, my Adam's apple is visible. I spend an afternoon on high alert, afraid that someone might notice one of my masculine features.

How many parks, men, and neighbours does it take to forget someone?

I get carried away by hearts at the end of texts. I get carried away by an emoji sent by someone I barely know and whom I forget within seconds.

I think about the Brazilian trans woman who was filmed, the video put up on the Internet. She was beaten up and then thrown into a wheelbarrow, which was later dumped in a ditch, the way people dispose of dead leaves in the fall.

"Don't bother yourself about the wine, okay?" this man tells me. "It all tastes the same."

I stop myself from telling him that, actually, it's men that all taste the same.

In their arms, I find my scaffolding; I choose to be the woman they want, to make sure that they don't reject me. Sometimes, I ask too many questions and it annoys them. I tell them I'm sorry, in this accent that betrays my birthplace, and I feed the fear that they'll discover that I am a fugitive of circumstances that were out of my control.

They press themselves against my body in the hopes of getting a little bit of love. I let them believe what they want to believe because I know they won't stay in my life. I think about all the girls that have broken them too. I think about our porcelain bodies broken and glued back together, broken, and glued back together, that make love in a roar of debauchery. We imagine things—*Oh, it would be perfect, taking a little pontoon along the shore*—to tell ourselves we're romantic, before devouring each other. We surrender to the most fragile of ideas.

Sometimes, they leave me traces of their passing: a scratch, a bite mark, a bruise. I know then that I didn't dream it. I go into their bathrooms, often when they are knocked out by the *too much* love that I have, or the deadly full-on rage of my grief, and I hold on to the counter, but my body leaks from itself, slides down the drain of what will hopefully be a quick shower. I am not empty, I promise you; I am filled with anti-love.

They reassure me of my femininity and my validity as a woman.

I think about the trans woman murdered on New Year's Day.

I watch them cook me meals while their hips sway, as though they are genuinely happy I'm there, in their lives, registering like a blooming bud. My smile hurts. It shows that I'm passing up something that could exist. I tell myself that at least I know a little more of life after having tasted their sweat.

I think about the trans woman who was murdered, stabbed with a knife and fork by her husband, who lost his temper.

I am desirable only at the time of sexual gymnastics. I beg for sweat with a fervour I didn't know I had. Fervour and fury are two words that resemble each other and become synonymous when you add alcohol to the mix.

I think about the trans woman burned alive in her car.

Sometimes, I don't feel like spreading my legs, I'd rather open up my heart, but then I do it anyways, because I didn't wear makeup, do my hair, and dress up for nothing, and I'm not emerging from my lethargy for nothing either. I find my self-esteem at the back of their throats and they a reason to live for a night at the back of mine.

In the morning, they cook me eggs which are scrambled, just like our relationship. Our silences slip like excuses. The phone numbers rain down; for once, it's not me crying. I mix up their names, so now I call everyone "you."

You are not him.

You are not there.

Through them I speak to Guillaume.

The city is different when I look at it from their French doors. The seasons pass across my stomach, crooked. Guillaume's absence takes over me.

"You're a trans girl but you don't look it."

It doesn't look like I want to die either, and yet.

I think about the trans woman whose eye was gouged out and who was stabbed dozens of times before being left in the sun at the mercy of vultures.

I get a quartz tattooed on the inside of my arm. I become mineral, my edges now sharp and glaring. I search for the gaze that will make me solid. If I can't recognize at least a little bit of Guillaume's tenderness in their eyes, I end up running away while they sleep.

I think about the trans woman beaten up on a bus in Veracruz.

Some don't say a single thing all night. This is how I recognize those who are only interested in me for the unique experience of my woman's penis. I would like to have love for them, would like to be strong enough to enlighten their consciousness to the truth. I would like to have enough time to teach them that inside this body hides a heart.

People party hard in Montreal, every day of the week. Sometimes, I pass by the bar that Guillaume and I once went to. I see that young man on the roof of the building, who takes the hand of the man he'll spend a pivotal period of his life with. I think about them, that pair who take in the entire night with their young, enthusiastic mouths and bring it back to the foot of the bed where they live their life for two, and all the beauty that will emerge from their relationship.

People start to know my name at some of the bars. I'm the girl who always drinks an apricot brandy in memory of her faraway friend. It's the trans girl, watch out, she'll trick you, my guy. It's the girl who cries about her assault on the shoulders of daddies. It's the girl who breaks out in Barbara's "Dis, quand reviendras-tu?" or who, at last call, sings Joe Dassin's "Dans les yeux d'Émilie" to the doorman until he tells her to go to bed. She is a jukebox filled with tears. A girl who believes she arrived too late to her own life.

I think about the trans woman left to die in a ravine, face swollen, her skirt raised to show the world the hatred of the other.

Sometimes, to my own astonishment, I don't get wasted or go home with a man. I act sensibly and go home early. Even though I'm an adult and fully grown, I still have to ask for directions. I wander St-Denis; it's packed with people, as many as in my head. I try to find the poetry in people running on the sidewalk. It's often nothing more than people running on the sidewalk.

Each fall, I envy the Canada geese that take flight to greener pastures. I can't flee my life without getting rid of myself.

I hold on to the few precious mornings to keep going. When the day's sunbeams shine through the curtains to flood our naked and dripping bodies. The cars hum, the kids have been resuscitated from the night. Everything can function. When I'm asked about my family, I feel uneasy. I don't know how to broach the topic of my family splitting up, relegating us to the four corners of the province. Instead, I talk about Japanese anime, dogs, cats, crystals, diamonds born of high pressure. I cling to their smiles. If one day I can reach at least one of their hearts, I won't have lived for nothing.

I think about the trans woman who was kidnapped and strangled.

I fall asleep after aligning myself with their breathing. When we wake up, we admire the shadows of passersby heading to their jobs projected onto the wall; it's possible to admire life as it continues without us.

I look them right in the eye and lightning bolts pass through my retinas into theirs without tearing apart what we're living. A lightning bolt can last for just a morning.

I try to imagine what a couple's life might look like.

I see myself in a sunny kitchen. The "I love you's" crossed across the breakfast table don't fade before landing.

When they live on the fifteenth floor in a chic neigh bourhood, it puts things into perspective. The people below look like ants. I ask myself if one tear, falling from this height, could pick up enough speed to kill someone.

They often end up telling me that it's not my fault that the relationship has dissolved; it's only because they need a vagina to satisfy them sexually. I get used to the slamming doors, again.

I think about this Chinese trans woman who was killed by teenagers.

Sometimes they invite me on trips. I know that neither the caviar nor the chlorinated pools will pull me out of my despair. I know that no matter the destination, I will have to confront my childhood in any language imaginable. I borrow their hearts because I never learned how to find my own. Several questions await their responses: for starters, how does one remain standing when she's an expatriate of her own childhood?

It's hard to advance from one human heatwave to the next without it feeling like a prison sentence. They won't cease to remind me, after having scrutinized my body with a magnifying glass, that I don't have any birthmarks.

"It's because my existence isn't meant to be acknowledged. I am a deportee of the cosmos."

I am the only one who laughs, and it's often a sign that I should leave.

I think about the trans man who was killed by two women he put up in his home.

The smell of dishes conceived in lovers' kitchens makes me think of their love. I hope that this period of love walking on eggshells is drawing to an end. I try to recognize the woman dragged down by alcohol who stares at me in the mirrors of restaurant bathrooms. I think about everything I'm hiding: my sadness, my doll under my pillow. Sometimes I cry when the bartender refuses to serve me because I've had too much to drink. I no longer know where to put myself; I'm a star that's flying across too many skies at once.

I learn to appreciate the taxi rides through the city when I return to my apartment or, rather, my cabin in the trees, as I like to call it. The poetry of this stateless bubble becomes familiar. Whether day or night, these journeys send me into a particular meditative state that I don't allow myself to get into anywhere else. Evenings and nighttime favour melancholy. I think about what my family would have looked like if I weren't a trans woman. Sometimes I start to cry, hoping that my tears taste like the river from the childhood that I've cowardly abandoned.

I smile at men out of courtesy, the same way you smile at someone you don't really want to know. I smile to cover up my face. In the lead-up to another date, I hope this is the guy who can erase Guillaume from my heart, like dentists extract rotten teeth.

It surprises them when I ask them to hit me and, after only one or two strikes, I burst into tears. I have to bury him under other bodies, other smells, other pains. It's in pain that I shine, it's in pain that I take my place in the firmament. They offer me whiskey, no ice, and I show them my softest face. I soak myself in their skins to save my own. I sometimes dread the pair of high heels in the entrance that aren't mine but the harbinger of an emotional disaster. I no longer know what the world is like; I've cut myself off from it for I don't know how long. I merely exist, with splinters and my colossal sadness.

I think about the trans woman sex worker in Mexico City shot and killed by one of her clients.

I tell myself I should be in a psych's office, not between their legs. They secretly like that their chests become a cradle for my fatigue and my disenchantment. We like to believe in this security offered one evening when we've drunk a glass too many of rum. We like to collect the things that the sea has thrown back upon the shore. I remember the woods that welcomed me without judgment, that instead offered to hold my hand, all those outstretched hands, intangible, offered out of habit and not love. I remember the dirt path that gave way to the heart of a mysterious forest and that hypnotized me to the point where, one beautiful school day, I fell from the top of a fence. I think about the village that I promised myself I'd build under the fir trees. Of all the incapacitated who wait for me in my weak promise and who for a decade have not found a way to clip their roots. I think about the car accident, of lives so fragile, and of relationships that are even more so. Of the effusion of sad sperm. Of the soaked pillows from too-long nights. Of the tenacity of bees on the carcasses of flowers.

"Alright, I'm going to come. Turn around. Your dick is stopping me from coming."

Sometimes I kick them out, angry, and yet I'm mad at myself.

My lovers can't be spontaneous. They are the product of programming. They depend on the phases of the moon. They rely on the calendar.

I emerge from their rooms after having spent a night wrapped in their arms and their silences. In the street, the sun causes me to squint. I never really return home. I'm in an all-men's land. And yet I never land anywhere. For months now, all I do is dig myself into their beds so as to not be alone. I want to keep myself away from what's killing me, but how do I get distance from myself?

Sometimes, I think it would be easier to drown myself, to hang myself, or to shoot myself. In these moments, I plunge into their mouths headfirst and I'm relieved to no longer have to think about anything. I bury my face in their furry chests, this habitable forest, and I thank them for being temporary places to land.

I would like to seize the present moment with the same vigour and greed as the seagulls that sometimes interrupted our picnics at the beach.

Sometimes, there's no music at their places, only silence. I have the time to feel bad for my mom, who helps pay my rent because I only work part-time in a small drugstore in Hochelaga. In this silence, I hear myself think and panic.

I drag them with me into the depths of my depression. Disappointment comes when I understand that neither they nor anyone else can teach me how to unite with the world.

I hang on to my reflection in boutique windows. I'm searching for proof that I exist. I envy people who don't have to do that. I have to find myself, exert all my efforts like they do when searching for missing children.

I think about the trans woman murdered in India.

Maybe it's me that I'm trying to meet behind the moustaches, shirt collars buttoned up to the neck, tattoos. Maybe it's me that I'm trying to find under the wax crayons scattered on the table, behind the kids who have to be picked up at four o'clock sharp, or behind the woman who knows. We have, on occasion, created a love monster who cries behind a hurt child's eyes. We have created pipe dreams in every place we've passed through.

I wander through an underground city, from subway car to subway car, covered up to my knees, my eyebrows furrowed. They love me from nine to four. Even if we take off our shoes, we always end up dirtying the house. When I get home, I wonder if my love of blue jays and bears might have been more fulfilling than the love they offered. I feel like we should have a psychiatrist assigned to us at birth, right when we come out of our mothers, or at least the first time we ever get punched by life.

I wonder why another person's heat is so crucial to me when I spent my childhood in glacial river waters. I ask myself where the wall will be built and if it'll be high enough to discourage me.

They leave me in the hollows of their palms. They don't really get me. They only know that I'm fragile. They push me into a taxi. "Get her home safe." And they pray secretly that I don't dirty the inside of the car. I still want to be with you, crying this nameless sadness that brings us back to the vain anonymity of our desires. We are anonymous so we don't get too attached, so we don't develop a taste for it. There has to be someone behind the masks. I would like to forget you. That you would slide off me like pearly water off a duck's feathers. It's unfair that one single encounter can stay with me for the rest of my life.

I think about my bony hands that try to keep them back. The cracking of bones at dawn. I think about my resurrection in the park, of the sounds of dogs barking and the joggers struggling, breathless. I think about the grains of sand encrusted in the thighs of encounters. About the sound of wounds that open to reveal responses.

I don't know how many times they've returned me demanding a refund, how many times I've answered to my name with canine enthusiasm. I also have the ardour of a cat, the need to leave when they try to take me. I think about the letters I write them to keep them close to me, about the tears between words, between lines, about the faces deforming in the rain, about the cries we no longer hear out of habit. I think about the coat collar we hold on to, to push back the moment of departure. I think about knees before they're scratched by cement, that bleed from the despondency of cities and the weariness of the countryside.

I think of all these bored and wounded men who have added to my worries and my injuries. I don't want anything to do with anyone while my heart is so badly opened. I'm ripe with familiarity. With the desire to speak with someone who understands me, with someone who'll listen. My psych tells me I have issues with men, that I can't let them go. I understand the reason for the tissue box and the table between us. I show her that, yes, I can do without them. I just need to relearn how to speak, how to not take on their voices. This is also what I did with female personification: I took the voice of others because I was too afraid of my own. Yes, I can do without them, dear psych. I go to the drugstore to buy cat litter. It reassures me to see her rush to relieve herself on clean litter. I know how to find pleasure in a bowl of ramen and jalapeno pepper sardines with a tea biscuit dipped in honey. Alone, I spice up my redneck tastes. I'm certain this makes me a girl capable of doing without men.

One day I wake up, more certain than ever. It's in reaching rock bottom that we bounce back. I am a woman without compromise. Worthy of being in my lover's bedroom or my in-laws' sunny living room. I will no longer be the third-wheel woman, the girl who is a wallflower to beautiful things, the girl in the cupboard; I will no longer be no one's or everyone's.

I start forgetting the places I meet them. I forget the heat waves and gradually get used to the autumn crops I've been nurturing. It is time for harvest. Finally, I realize that they weren't able to break my heart because I didn't have one. I remember that they would cover me with a sheet when I slept over, like a mortician, and especially that one of them took me by the throat to kiss me. I grabbed him by the throat in turn to make sure that it was him, the end of the world.

I often cross paths with a guy in my neighbourhood who looks like my childhood friend Mathias, or at least, like the idea I have of him as an adult. So much has happened since our escapades. We never took the time to stay in touch. The snow covered our childhoods a hundred times over, and we let the terrain go wild.

The moon's light slides over my body shivering from missing men and from the rotten woods of my conscience. I realize that Guillaume didn't just leave me once but that I experienced his departure every time one of those men left me.

I don't know the path to get home; I only know the path leading to sorrow. It's reassuring in a certain way, to think that we're going somewhere.

I take pills to help me sleep. I get back in contact with Manon, my mom's cousin who Olivier and I stayed with when we were younger. On the phone she says, "Do you remember when you were a little girl? You must have been ten or eleven. When guests came over, you would run away into the woods. We had to look for you so many times." I respond that it's time for me to come out of those woods. I think back to that dog that used to come see me, and I wonder if he's still alive. I tell myself that at the very least, the moments we spent together live on.

How many mirrors do I have to pass through before finally reaching myself? How is it possible to live so long deprived of a father and mother? How did Olivier and I, one night, after our parents fought, end up without any genealogy?

I take.
I throw away.
I build.
I destroy.
I feel my breasts, looking for the tumour of childhood.

One late spring morning, the phone rings.

"Hello, my b—… my girl."

Her voice is trembling.

"What's going on?"

"Your grandmother passed away this morning."

My breath stops short. I hyperventilate. Something to hold on to, the corner of the table, the back of a chair, the edge of the bed, anything. I slide all over the place.

"No no no no no no, it's not possible, you have to be lying, stop it."

I breathe in, implode, I tumble back with the force of the news and my bedroom wall catches my fall. I collapse onto the floor. It's not possible that my grandmother has died.

"The funeral is going to be in three weeks. We're expecting you."

She hangs up right after, and I double over in pain. It takes me a minute to understand that she's no longer on the other end of the line.

Grandma, where are they—our red fingers, red from raspberries picked for tarts, stains on our aprons that look like improvised animal silhouettes? My childhood comes back to me, takes me by the hand, and insists on catching up on lost time.

One day, later on, I get another call, this time from my big brother Olivier.

"Hello?"

"…"

"Hello?"

"…"

"Is it you?"

"More than ever."

We talk about how much we miss our grandmother.

Later: "I always knew you weren't a boy like the others. I can hear in your voice that you're happy."

"What does it feel like to learn that you don't have a brother anymore?"

"We lived our childhood as boys; I had a little brother but that doesn't stop me from having a sister. Who I'm excited to meet, by the way."

We cry together. I can hear Olivier's breath through the receiver. This is what life is made of: departures, arrivals, returns, like the waves of a river.

"See you soon, sister."

I, who had planned to write a suicide note, learn that my brother is going to be a dad. Life persists in keeping me here.

I vent to Steph. When the funeral date approaches, I decide to go see him in Québec City so that we can make the trip back to my hometown together. We pass by my grandmother's lilacs, the lilacs now blooming without her. It's time to head to the birthplace of my sadness. Steph is dressed up in flamboyant colours to "represent the real you, my dear," and I like that he teaches me how to see in colour.

"I missed you, bitch! Let's do this. And after, promise me you'll at least come back and perform."

"I promise!"

Look at me finding the will to make promises.

The car devours the kilometres and we sing along at the top of our lungs to Britney Spears, The Cardigans, Beyoncé, Shakira, our throats flowering with the scent of lilacs. We talk about the times we would sleep on the floor of the living room, so exhausted from the joy of nights hanging out. I forgive myself for the hasty urge that pushed me to escape like a deer inhabited with the fear of being eaten. The sun is spectacular again. Steph taps on the steering wheel to the rhythm of the music. It's weird to think that I'm going to my grandmother's funeral in this state of mind. In a way, she has brought us all together.

Suddenly, I realize that I'm emerging from the depths

of the earth like Persephone coming back in spring. I'm going to relearn how to live to the beat of dinner gatherings, to music played in the living room and shared laughter. There will no longer be a question of escaping myself.

I get excited when I see the asphalt shingles of the roof. It's like looking at the head of a baby emerging from their mother's womb. My family home appears from behind trees that have gotten bigger since I last saw them. It's the first time I've come back to the village in years. My lungs fill with air that reminds me of playing in the woods; I think I hear the sound of two brothers laughing under the ash trees.

We enter the gravel driveway. Nothing has changed. My mom is on her knees in the flowerbed planting dahlias that she encircles with daisies. Her movements are a little slower than when I was a kid, but she has that same irreproachable energy and focus. She still has that big hat that she used to wear at the beach during our trips to the river, and I've kept my smile for her; I hadn't realized. Bernard stands behind her, holding a bag of fertilizer. They exchange a look. A smile. They still love each other.

Farther away, near the shed, my dad is with a woman; I don't know if it's the same woman he was with when we were younger. He's laughing like he did in the blueberry field; he didn't forget this sun, one might say. He hugs his girlfriend and kisses her on the forehead. I believe in daydreams. Olivier is there too. He's the biggest in the family now. Long hair tied up in a bun at the top of his head "as though you're not tall enough as is," my mom would later say. Olivier is with a woman with a full-moon belly. She has cheeks rounded with happiness. I feel like a stranger to all this life that has gone on without me. Maybe this is all a hallucination. I'm afraid of what I stand to lose. A rectangular table, already set, has been arranged in front of the house. Olivier goes to the barbecue, turns over pieces of meat and checks the foil-covered vegetables while whistling. He used to be meagre; he's now burly, more like our dad.

They wait till we get out of the car. An intense heat grows insistent in my chest.

"I don't know if I can do it, Steph, I don't know. No, turn around. We'll go to Montreal, okay? No, I don't want to."

"How many things have you done that you thought you'd never be able to do? In the end, you've talked about those things with pride... You haven't done hundreds of kilometres today to just turn back, really. Girl, it's not like you killed anyone. In fact, you gave birth to the girl who was waiting on death's door." He takes me by the shoulders. "We don't choose the families we're born into, but we can choose to love them ... differently, better, you name it. They wouldn't have invited you if they didn't accept you."

What Steph is saying makes me cry, all while propelling me forward with rare confidence. I unlock the door. I have my hand on the door handle.

The car's tinted windows keep me shrouded in mystery for a few more seconds. I pull out a mirror from my purse to see if I'm still here, but I barely look at myself, and put it away immediately. No, I don't need to look at myself.

I walk out in broad daylight. Here she is, the lost child. I'm no longer just a voice on the other end of the line. I'm here so we can love each other better, so they can understand me in my wholeness, as I am really. Mom drops her gardening tools and hurries towards me. She hugs me so hard that I feel like my blood has stopped.

"It was you then, all these years…" she says, while staring deeply into my eyes.

Our tears mingle as we sigh in relief. I am still alive, and that boy dead in my stomach has flowered, watered by his own tears. I am still standing, Mom, despite contrary winds, despite fights, despite rages and furies. Mom, I've had enough of losing myself in others and for others. I broke through the snow, Mom, and I can breathe.

She holds my face in her hands. I've missed you so much, Mom.

"You are so beautiful, my girl. We lost each other, only to be reunited, closer than ever. It's your grandmother who arranged this, that cunning little lady."

She kisses me on the forehead for a long time. Steph gets out of the car and says hello. Olivier and my dad come over to us. My dad is a bit cold. But he's here, finally. All the sentences from his postcards were dictating the poem of his return. My voice trembling and my shoulders curved timidly. I dare to say, "Dad, I missed you."

He doesn't say anything. He pulls me towards him. He hugs me for a whole minute and it's the most touching of apologies. Time will sort things out. I don't feel like forcing it. Olivier joins the hug, and my mother does too, to complete the atom. They look at each other for a second, my mother and father, and I think I can see them from when I was younger, exchanging that precious and luminous look. Then they break into laughter. Bernard plays some music on the stereo. Joe Dassin's warm voice envelops our hug. My heart is beating quickly. We sit at the table to eat.

I sing with Joe Dassin. "I had the sun, the night, and the day in the eyes of love."

Later on, having talked about my life in Montreal and Québec City, I sit with my back against a tree in the yard. My dad comes to join me. We don't know what to say to each other.

"I wasn't always present in your life, and know that I regret that things didn't go the way I would have wanted them to. I was really hard on you because I couldn't accept that you were different… that you were a girl. I know this won't make up for lost time but—your grandmother and I, we saw each other not long ago, and that day, we were in a thrift store, and we found this."

He searches his pocket and takes out a charm. It's a house, and it resembles ours.

"I thought you could put it with your rose quartz heart. It'll be pretty."

Tears trickle down my cheeks. He hugs me. Mom looks at us with tenderness. A tear escapes her eye.

I realize that even though time and life have separated us, we have never stopped loving each other. I look at them, one by one, and give them my first real smile. They're all here. I'm here. I think about that little girl who so wanted to know what was hidden at the edge of the horizon. I tell her that, in the end, there's always another, it never ends. And it's perfect this way.

My family dances. I stay at the picnic table, a pencil in hand.

Once, a girl from a village at the edge of a river finally decided to live for herself.

ACKNOWLEDGEMENTS

Gabrielle Boulianne-Tremblay

Bertrand Laverdure, for guiding me through the winds and the tides. Jade Bérubé, for patience with this colossal project and for good advice. Mélanie Vincelette, my editor at Marchand de feuilles, for listening and hearing my heartbeat. Les Éditions marchand de feuilles, for the trust. Nicolas Fiset, for having seen this little light that really exists.

Annie Pronovost and Roger Des Roches, for their talent as goldsmiths, and all those who have directly or indirectly supported the writing of this novel over the years:

Danielle Boulianne, Gilbert Tremblay, Francesca Tremblay, Karenne Tremblay, David Rochette, Elly-Jade Rochette, Emma Lanteigne, Pascale Cormier, Jade Cormier, Pascale Bérubé, Élise Drolet-Turcotte, Joseph Elliott Israël Gorman, Alexandre Turgeon-Dalpé, Alexandre G. Vermeil, Benjamin Lachance, Denis S., Hélène Imbeault, Annabelle Drolet, Amélie Jetté, Bobby Raymond, Simon Carrière, Busque, Sonia Girard, Denis Tremblay, Marc-André Tremblay, Maxime Tellier, Robin Noureau, Mimi, Alex Tremblay, Julie Tremblay, Yvette Tremblay, Jean-Claude Boulianne, Serge Boulianne, Marie-Marcelle Godbout, Ro Lemire, Maya, Si Poirier, Katiane, Julie Poirier, Christopher Tremblay, Fléchanne Fortin, Sara Hébert.

Also special thanks to the people behind the English edition:

Dimitri Nasrallah, thank you for welcoming my story in a language where it can bloom again, and for having seen the truth in this dandelion.

Simon Dardick, co-publisher of Vehicule Press, a publisher that welcomes authenticity in such a heartwarming way.

David Drummond for the cover.

And a very special thanks to Eli Tareq El Bechelany-Lynch for this wonderful translation.

ACKNOWLEDGEMENTS

Eli Tareq El Bechelany-Lynch

I would like to thank Dimitri Nasrallah for thinking of me for this book, for being a thorough editor, and for helping me with my first book-length translation. Thank you to Simon Dardick for all the less visible work that goes into publishing a book together.

Thank you, Gabrielle, for trusting me with your lovely book and for being a delight to work with.

Thank you to everyone who listened to me talk through the jigsaw puzzle that is translation and who championed me during this past year, including Felix, Lee, Samia, and Shae.

ESPLANADE
Books

A House by the Sea : A novel by Sikeena Karmali
A Short Journey by Car : Stories by Liam Durcan
Seventeen Tomatoes : Tales from Kashmir : Stories by Jaspreet Singh
Garbage Head : A novel by Christopher Willard
The Rent Collector : A novel by B. Glen Rotchin
Dead Man's Float : A novel by Nicholas Maes
Optique : Stories by Clayton Bailey
Out of Cleveland : Stories by Lolette Kuby
Pardon Our Monsters : Stories by Andrew Hood
Chef : A novel by Jaspreet Singh
Orfeo : A novel by Hans-Jürgen Greif
[Translated from the French by Fred A. Reed]
Anna's Shadow : A novel by David Manicom
Sundre : A novel by Christopher Willard
Animals : A novel by Don LePan
Writing Personals : A novel by Lolette Kuby
Niko : A novel by Dimitri Nasrallah
Stopping for Strangers : Stories by Daniel Griffin
The Love Monster : A novel by Missy Marston
A Message for the Emperor : A novel by Mark Frutkin
New Tab : A novel by Guillaume Morissette
Swing in the House : Stories by Anita Anand
Breathing Lessons : A novel by Andy Sinclair
Ex-Yu : Stories by Josip Novakovich
The Goddess of Fireflies : A novel by Geneviève Pettersen
[Translated from the French by Neil Smith]
All That Sang : A novella by Lydia Perović
Hungary-Hollywood Express : A novel by Éric Plamondon
[Translated from the French by Dimitri Nasrallah]